A DANGEROUS DEPARTURE FROM HILLBILLY HOLLOW

BLYTHE BAKER

There's a new ghost in town...and it's calling Emma away from Hillbilly Hollow.

A ghostly visit from her former landlady draws Emma away from sleepy little Hillbilly Hollow to investigate a murder in the big city. But what seems like a straightforward case soon becomes entangled with an event from Emma's past and a personal quest for justice.

1

I'd avoided my grandparents' farm for years after I went off to college and then moved to New York City, but it was amazing how even after all that time away, I could be back for a few months and it already felt like home again. Grandma had shouted up the attic stairs to wake me up just as the sun was peeking over the horizon that Saturday morning, and after stuffing me with eggs and bacon, had dragged me out to her vegetable garden to help harvest squash and pumpkins. We'd been out there most of the day.

With dirt up to my elbows and sweat across my brow, I thought about what I'd be doing if I was still in New York. I probably would have slept until mid-morning and then walked down to the bakery on the corner for a warm bagel and a cup of coffee. Then, I would have done some shopping or caught up on some graphic design work at home. The ad agency where I'd had my old job had provided the kind of work I could often take home with me. As I thought about it, I couldn't lie, that all sounded nice. But it was also nice doing a bit of physical labor.

"Are you really going to let an old woman beat you,

Emma?" Grandma asked from the vegetable row next to me. I'd been too deep in my thoughts to notice, but she had pulled ahead and had nearly filled her wooden basket with butternut squash.

I put my head down and began working faster. "Never! I just wanted to give you a fighting chance."

She laughed and shook her head, no doubt knowing I couldn't back down from a challenge and now at my new pace we'd be done twenty minutes sooner.

Originally, I hadn't expected to be in Hillbilly Hollow for long, but now that I was settled, it was impossible to imagine going back to my old life in the city. Having my grandparents around was nice. I was able to keep an eye on them and make sure everything was okay. They were both spry and healthy for their age, but I still worried about them. Plus, being back with my childhood friends, Billy and Suzy, had been fun. I had friends in New York, of course, but everyone always seemed so busy there—rushing off for appointments and shows. But Billy and Suzy could always make time for a hang out session or dinner at the diner.

I'd become so comfortable being back home, in fact, that sometimes it was easy to forget the reason I'd originally come back. Dr. Jenson, back in New York, thought being out on the family farm, away from the hustle and bustle of the city, would help me heal after being struck by a taxi. He thought it would help make the visions I'd been seeing go away. In his opinion, the ghostly apparitions were nothing more than the misfiring of electrical impulses in my brain after the trauma to my head from the accident.

After finally talking to Grandma and Grandpa about my visions, though, I had finally decided they weren't misfirings at all. But rather, the blow to the head had opened my eyes to things most people couldn't see. This seemed increasingly likely since, according to Grandma and Grandpa, several members of my family had experienced similar visions after head trauma. If it wasn't for this information, I would have thought I was crazy, especially after Preacher Jacob appeared to me after his murder and helped me solve the crime. He'd even saved my life when his murderer had tried to make me his second victim. It all seemed insane, but armed with my family history, I now knew that I had a special gift—the ability to communicate with the dead and, sometimes, help them find peace.

"Aha!"

I looked up to see my grandma doing her approximation of a celebration dance, arms raised over her head, knees bobbing back and forth. She was at the end of her row and I, once again, had gotten lost in my own head and was barely even three-fourths of the way done.

"Well done," I said, clapping for her and shaking my head in mock disappointment.

She laughed and wiped her forehead with a floral tea towel before walking down my row and kneeling in the dirt next to me. "Lucky for you, I'm not a sore winner."

Together, we had everything in the garden harvested in the next twenty minutes.

"What are we going to do with all of these pumpkins?" I asked. "None of them are big enough for any competitions."

"Pie, of course," Grandma said. "Margene Huffler made a pumpkin pie last October and by the way the ladies in the Quilting Circle went on and on about it, you would have thought she'd cured a disease. Apparently, Margene grinds her own spices. Well, I can do better than that. I'm going to grind my own spices *and* use a garden-grown pumpkin."

"I'm sure it will leave Mrs. Huffler's pie in the dirt," I said with a laugh.

Then I sobered for a second. I actually felt bad for the Huffler family—and not just because Margene's pie was about to be bested by my grandma's. The Hufflers had been through a lot lately. Margene's daughter, Prudence, had been in love with the murdered Preacher Jacob. Then Prudence herself had nearly been the victim of another crime. She had survived the attempt on her life but must have been shaken by it because, shortly afterward, she had packed up and left town. No doubt, Margene would be lonely without her, but I hoped Prudence made a success of whatever new life she built for herself.

Grandma's forehead was wrinkling in concern. "Where's Snowball?"

I looked around, expecting to see a furry little tail somewhere nearby, but instead saw nothing but a small hole where Snowball had been digging in the dirt. "I'm not sure. She usually doesn't wander too far."

"The clouds look heavy with rain, and it's supposed to get a bit chilly tonight, so you'll want to find her. I can finish cleaning up here," Grandma said.

"Are you sure? I don't mind helping."

Grandma grabbed the shovel out of my hand and shooed me away with her dirt-covered gardening glove. "I'm old, not helpless. Besides, I don't mind that old nanny goat sleeping in the house with you, but she'll stink to high Heavens if she gets rained on. So, unless you want to give her a bath in the basin next to the outhouse, you better find her quick.

That was enough of a threat to get me going. I hopped over the low wire fence that helped keep the rabbits out of the garden and took off in the direction of the back field.

Grandma was right. I hadn't noticed, but fleecy gray clouds had rolled in and the air felt thick and damp. A chill ran down my back, and I chalked it up to the sudden chill. It also could have been that I was standing in the exact same spot I'd been in when I'd first seen Preach Jacob's spirit after his murder, but I decided not to think about that.

"Snowball!" I'd never figured out whether Snowball could understand her name or, even if she could, whether she'd always respond to it. But she had proven herself to be mostly like a dog in every other respect, so I thought it was worth a try. "Snowball!"

Something white off at the far end of the field caught my eye, and I turned quickly, but nothing was there. Tingles worked their way from the base of my neck to the top of my head, and I rolled my head in a circle to dispel them. Everything was fine. I was just keyed up from running across the field and my body was confusing endorphins for adrenaline. Or something like that.

Another flash of movement made me turn the other direction, and suddenly the chill in the air didn't feel so natural. Could it really be this cool in early autumn? It had come on suddenly, too. A bit too suddenly. And Snowball was probably waiting for me up at the house. She had never taken off into the field by herself before, so I didn't know why I'd assumed she'd do so now. As I turned back towards the house, a final glimpse of white drew my attention. I turned to the right and saw, plain as day, the silvery outline of a woman.

Startled, I stumbled backwards, tripping over a rock and falling on my backside. I scrambled to my feet again, never once taking my eyes off of the apparition. I could see the horizon through the apparition as though it was a foggy glass window, but I could also see the distinct womanly shape. She was plump and wearing an ankle-length dress, but otherwise the features weren't clear. Still, something about her looked familiar.

I started to step forward to investigate, hoping I could discover her identity, when I heard a shrill bleat and then a fifty-pound goat hurled itself at my chest. Once again, I found myself backside in the dirt.

"Snowball," I said, a mixture of displeasure and relief in my voice.

She gave me a panicked "maw" and then buried her head under my arm. I wrapped my arms around her and managed to get us both up off the ground, but by the time I looked back to where the woman had been standing, there was nothing there.

"What on Earth are you doing all the way out here?" I asked as if I expected the nanny to respond. Snowball only looked up at me with wide eyes. Then, distant thunder rumbled, and she tucked herself further into my chest, a shivering shaking mess. "Let's get back to the farmhouse before we get soaked and you have a conniption."

2

B illy's truck was visible in the drive as soon as I
cleared the old wooden fence that surrounded the
back field. Though, he wasn't anywhere in sight.

"Grandma is probably stuffing him with biscuits and
honey in the kitchen," I whispered to Snowball, who
seemed to be calming down the further away we got from
the site of the apparition.

When I got a bit closer to the house, I dropped Snowball
on the ground and patted the woolly fluff above her tail.
"Now, go on, but don't get yourself into any trouble."

"If she's anything like you, that might be a little hard."

I looked up to see Billy Stone, or rather Dr. Will Stone,
smiling at me, his bright white teeth offset by his naturally
tan skin. Just as I'd expected, he was holding a biscuit that
was dripping in honey and leaning against the door to
Grandma and Grandpa's shack.

"I'm not sure what you mean. I never get into any
trouble."

He raised a dubious eyebrow at me and smiled.

"What brings you here?" I asked.

"You," he said, tipping his head towards me.

The simple answer made my face feel warm and my stomach fluttery. "Oh, really?"

"I saw Suzy and Brian heading to the diner and I thought I'd come pick you up for an impromptu meeting of the three musketeers."

"And Brian," I added, one finger raised in the air.

Billy laughed. "Yes, three musketeers and Brian."

I was just about to accept his invitation on the condition that my grandma didn't mind me skipping dinner with her and my grandfather when my phone let out a shrill ring in my pocket. The sound made me jump. Most everyone I talked to these days stopped by the house if they needed anything from me, just as Billy had done. Or they would text me, which was only one beep instead of the airhorn-style alarm going off now.

I gave Billy an apologetic smile, pulled my phone from my pocket, and took a few paces back towards the field to answer it.

"Hello?"

"Emma Hooper?" a disinterested male voice asked.

"This is her. Who am I speaking with?" I didn't recognize the voice and the number wasn't plugged into my phone.

"Jay Wilkins." A long pause ensued, the man clearly assuming I would recognize his name, which I absolutely didn't. "I'm Blanche Wilkins' son. I live in the basement of your building."

Suddenly, the image of a stout, freckled man with red hair and a seemingly endless supply of rock band t-shirts popped into my head. He was the son of my landlady in New York City. Blanche was the furthest thing from charming, and if possible, her son was even more off-putting. They both looked perpetually miserable and never had a smile for anyone. In Jay's defense, living in the basement of the apartment building his mother owned probably wasn't ideal. Of course, I was living in my grandparents' attic, but even my grandpa, who had a tendency to speak few words and contain his emotions, was a ray of bright sunshine in comparison to Blanche Wilkins. I definitely had the better living situation. But even now that I knew who was calling, it still didn't make any sense why Jay Wilkins would be calling me.

I had gone back to the city only once since making the move back to Missouri. I had returned just long enough to pack up a few things and look into giving up my apartment. In the end, I had ultimately decided to hang onto the place a little longer and put off moving my last few things to Missouri.

I was the ideal tenant, absent and paying regular rent for a place I hadn't even lived in for months. So, I didn't see why the son of my landlady would call me. And I couldn't begin to understand how he had even tracked down my phone number.

"Right, of course. Jay. How are you?" I asked, trying to disguise my confusion.

"Fine," he said quickly before getting down to business. "I'm calling to inform you that my mom has passed away very suddenly. I'm now the building's landlord. I was going to leave a sign under your door, but your neighbor told me you've been out of town for several months and it would be best to call you. So, I'm calling."

Had he just told me his mother died? Surely not. Yet, that was what he'd said. For clarification, I asked. "Your mother passed away?"

He sighed as if annoyed with me, and proceeded to

repeat everything he'd already said. "Yes, very suddenly, and that's made me your new landlord."

"I'm so sorry. She was such a lovely lady," I said.

"Yeah, sure," Jay said, not sounding at all convinced.

"I'm out of town these days," I said. "In Missouri." I didn't try to explain why I was still paying rent on an apartment I no longer lived in. I had decided some time ago to make Hillbilly Hollow my permanent home, but something in me had resisted completely giving up my old place.

Jay hummed disinterestedly. "It's no concern of mine. As long as rent is paid on time, you're free to do as you'd like. And since my mother didn't put up with late payments, I assume you've been paying on time and we won't have an issue."

"Yes, I always pay at the first of the month," I said. "But I really am so sorry to hear about your mother. I hope it was a peaceful passing."

"It seems like we understand each other, then. I have several more calls to make, so I really have to be going."

"Oh, yes, of course," I began, but before I could finish the thought, Jay interrupted.

"Goodbye, Miss Hooper." With that, he hung up.

I pocketed my phone and tried to draw up a mental image of Blanche Wilkins. The only times I saw her were if something was wrong with my rent payment or if we happened to run into one another in the hallway. And in those situations, I typically tried to squeeze by her without drawing too much attention to myself because the woman could talk, and none of her conversations were particularly cheerful. But now I wished I'd taken a better look at her. Could she have been the spirit I'd seen in the field? I didn't know the rules on ghosts, but the trip from New York City to Hillbilly Hollow, Missouri was a long one. Was that even possible? And if it was, why would she have come to see me? Why not drop in and torment her son. He was just a few floors down in the basement, after all.

"Who was that?"

I spun around, having nearly forgotten Billy was standing behind me.

"My New York landlady's son."

He raised both eyebrows. "Are you particularly close with your landlady's son?"

Was that a hint of jealousy or was I imagining it?

I let out a nervous laugh. "No, not at all. That may have been the first time we'd ever spoken. He called because my landlady is dead."

Billy's face fell, his tan skin taking on an ashen color. "I'm sorry."

I waved him away. "Thank you, but I didn't really know her."

"Know who, dear?" Grandma came outside with a checkered tea cloth holding what had to be a bundle of biscuits. She handed them to Billy along with a jar of her raspberry jam.

"Her landlady died," Billy said, answering for me.

"I'm so sorry, Emma. What happened?" Grandma moved closer and pulled me into a bone crushing hug. The woman was old, but certainly not frail.

I extricated myself and gave her an "everything is fine" smile. "Her son didn't say. And like I said, I didn't know her. Jay was only calling to tell me that he is now the building's landlord. Even he didn't seem too broken up about it all."

"That settles it. You've had a friend die, so now you have to let me take you out for a burger and a pop. It's the only right thing to do," Billy said, winking at me.

"Oh, that sounds fun," Grandma said, clapping her hands together.

"I know I was supposed to have dinner with you and Grandpa—"

Grandma shook her head and shooed me away. "Nonsense, child. You need to spend time with people your own age. Your grandpa and me are accustomed to our own company. We'll be fine without you. Go with Billy and don't hurry back."

"If you're sure," I said, narrowing my eyes at her.

"Positive. Get out of here before I throw you out." She blew me a kiss and disappeared back inside.

She seemed oddly happy about getting rid of me. Either she was relieved to spend an evening without me around or she was going to join my best friend Suzy in trying to push me into a relationship with Billy. Honestly, could no one understand that we were just friends? We used to go bull frogging and fishing together. He saw me cry when I fell out of a tree and sprained my ankle, and I'd seen him drop to the ground like a bomb was coming when a bumblebee flew past his ear. We'd been through too many embarrassing childhood and teenage years to date now.

"Hop on in," Billy said. He was already in his truck and he reached across the seat to push my door open.

Regardless of everyone else's motivations, I was starving and hanging with Billy and Suzy was always a good time. Plus, I was anxious to forget about the specter I'd seen in the field.

3

Suzy and Brian were already sitting in a booth in the back corner when Billy and I arrived. They waved at us as we entered.

"Suzy. Brian," Billy tipped an imaginary hat to each of them as he ushered me into the booth and then slid in after me.

"Doctor Billy," Suzy said with a mischievous grin.

Billy turned to Brian with an unamused smile. "Do you think your wife will ever call me by my proper name?"

"I don't have much control in this situation." Brian laughed and leaned over to kiss Suzy's cheek.

It was still crazy to me how Brian Bailey, the high school and college football star who was known to break a lot of hearts, had turned into a devoted husband for Suzy Colton. Just one look at them and it was obvious how much they loved and doted on one another.

"I suppose I better get used to it," Billy said.

Suzy jumped and then narrowed her eyes at Billy, confirming my suspicion that he had kicked her under the table. It didn't seem to matter how old we got, when we were together, we acted like teenagers.

Suzy and Brian, in an attempt to show how incredibly mushy they could be, each got hamburgers and then a strawberry milkshake to split. I ordered a grilled cheese and a coke, and Billy ordered a bacon cheeseburger and chili cheese fries.

"Aren't you always the one reminding us about our clogged arteries?" I asked, elbowing him in the side.

"Hey, it's been a long day and I deserve it," Billy said. "Besides, I was thinking you could share the chili cheese fries with me."

"You sure know the way to a girl's heart, Doctor Stone." We laughed, and when I looked over at Suzy, she was waggling her eyebrows suggestively.

I quickly decided to change the subject. "How is Annie's wedding planning going?"

Ever since Suzy and Brian's recent wedding, the whole town seemed to have caught wedding fever. Suzy's younger sister, Annie, was now planning a Christmas wedding. Annie and I had never been super close, so I was a little surprised when she'd asked me to be a bridesmaid. Less surprising was the fact that she'd asked Suzy to manage the details. Bossy Suzy was a natural born planner of events.

Suzy groaned, even though I knew she secretly relished the task. "Don't remind me. Annie and I have a taste test for the cake at the bakery tomorrow and I'm still trying to find the perfect bridesmaid dress."

I gave her a confused look and she slapped her own forehead.

"Oh, I guess I completely forgot to tell you. Annie decided to let the bridesmaids pick their own dresses. Alison is shorter than you and me, Mackenzie has a bigger chest, and there isn't a bridesmaid dress on this planet that will work for all of us, so Annie decided to let us pick. It has to be navy. Otherwise, free reign."

Suzy had her own clothing boutique, and I trusted Annie to share her big sister's fashion sense, but being able to choose my own dress for the wedding was a huge weight off my shoulders. Bridesmaids dresses were notoriously unflattering, and choosing my own dress meant I'd avoid that downfall and be able to enjoy the wedding without worrying that I looked like the losing side of a 'Who Wore it Better?' poll.

"Maybe when you shop for a dress you can also buy me a suit," Billy said with a grumble.

As a friend of Annie's fiancé, he'd been pressed into acting as an usher.

"You have a suit. I saw you wear it at the funeral a few months back," I said.

There was a brief moment of awkwardness as we all remembered the funeral of Preacher Jacob, and the ensuing drama of me capturing his murderer and nearly being murdered myself.

Luckily, our food arrived at that very moment, giving us all a chance to pause and collect our thoughts. As soon as the waitress was gone, Billy shot an annoyed glance at Suzy and then sighed. "The sister of the bride has proclaimed that I can't wear my funeral suit to Annie's wedding. It's a fashion *faux pas*."

"I'm not a queen, Billy. I don't make proclamations. But I am your most fashionable friend, and I'm trying to keep you from looking like a dud at my sister's wedding," Suzy said.

I laughed and patted Billy's shoulder. "I'm sure I can find you something."

Billy brightened, as I took a huge bite of my Texas toast grilled cheese.

"Emma Hooper!"

I looked towards the sound of the voice and saw none other than Sheriff Larry Tucker walking towards our booth. He was in dark wash jeans and a light-wash denim shirt, and I realized it was one of the few times I'd seen him out of his Sheriff uniform since coming back to town. That plus his blonde hair and beard cropped short made him look more like a male model than a sheriff.

Unable to respond since I was still chewing the much too large bite I'd taken of my sandwich, I lifted one hand in a greeting.

Tucker and I had gotten to know one another better ever since the day I had solved the mystery of Prudence Huffler's almost-murder. Tucker had arrived on that scene just in time to see a bad guy attempt to push me off a roof but fall off himself instead. Since then, the sheriff and I had grabbed coffee a couple times to discuss the finished case.

"Hey Tucker," Suzy said. "You off tonight?"

Tucker looked down at his clothes as if he'd forgotten he wasn't in his uniform and then ran a hand through his short hair. "A Sheriff's never really off duty, but I'm out on the town tonight, as the kids say."

Suzy laughed. "You here alone?"

He looked from me to Billy and back again, suddenly seeming a bit nervous. "Well, I actually stopped by Emma's grandparents' place a little bit ago, but heard she was here at the diner."

I swallowed the mass of bread and cheese, took a swallow of pop, and coughed out a response. "You were at my house?"

True, Tuck and I had shared a friendly cup of coffee but he'd never visited me at home before. Why would he?

"I figured I'd see if you wanted to grab dinner and catch up," he said. "But it seems like you already had plans."

"Sure did," Billy said, scooting closer to me in the booth so our legs touched.

"Maybe another time," I said with a smile.

Tucker winked at me. "I'll stop by the farmhouse again soon."

"Sounds great, Tucker."

As soon as he left, the bell above the diner door ringing to announce his departure, Suzy lowered her head and raised her eyebrows at me. "What was that about?"

"What was what about?" I asked.

She continued to stare, refusing to let the subject go.

"I don't know," I said. "He just wants to catch up. Ever since I was nearly murdered on the roof of the church after your wedding, Tucker and I have been chatting a little. I think he feels like I was useful in catching the bad guy. And we were friends once."

"No, you weren't," Suzy said, shaking her head, a fry hanging between her fingers like a cigarette. "He was three years older than us in school. We never even talked to him."

"It was a date," Billy said. When we all turned to him, he ate another chili cheese fry and shrugged. "I work with Tucker at crime scenes enough to know when he's asking a woman out, and he was asking Emma out."

I was surprised at the idea, but then I realized it made sense. It had been vain of me to think Tucker had been seeking me out lately just because he admired my crime-solving skills. Strange as it was to think of, maybe he had somehow gotten the impression that I was into him. Whether he had or not, it at least looked like *he* was into *me*.

I lowered my head, embarrassed for some reason. Billy pushed the chili cheese fries closer to me, hitting my hand and making me look up. When our eyes met, he lifted half his mouth in a smile. "You better eat some of these before I finish them all."

"You better not!" I said, quickly grabbing a handful.

4

The drive back to the farm was much quieter than the drive to the diner. Billy hadn't said much since Tucker had crashed the party, and he seemed too deep in his thoughts for me to interrupt. After a few minutes, he turned down the country music on the radio and drummed his fingers nervously on the steering wheel.

"So," he said, breaking the silence. "Where are you and Tucker going to go on your date?"

I barked out a surprised laugh. "I'm not going on a date with him."

"You told him he could stop by the farmhouse soon," he said. "That sounds like a date to me."

"You stopped by the farmhouse today, so does that mean this is a date?" I asked.

Billy got very quiet, and I wondered whether I hadn't stepped in something. Maybe Billy was feeling awkward that I was insinuating we were on a date when really, we'd just gone to the same diner we'd always gone to for burgers and fries. I was over-thinking everything.

"Speaking of you coming to the farmhouse," I said, transitioning away from the topic of dates. "When you showed up earlier, I got the call from my landlady's son, right?"

He nodded, though he still looked preoccupied. "Right, the lady who died."

"Yeah, well just before that phone call, I'd been out in the field looking for Snowball, and I saw something."

"Saw what?" Billy asked.

I gave him a knowing look, and suddenly his eyes widened and he nodded his head. "You mean, like, a vision?"

I shrugged, not sure how much to tell him. All the previous times we'd talked about the visions, that's what he thought they were—hallucinations. If I ever confessed they were actual ghosts, I'd sound like a nut case.

"What did you see?" he asked.

I said, "I'm pretty sure I saw Blanche Wilkins, my landlady. It was before I even knew she'd died, but I would swear it was her. The figure I saw had on the same cotton, ankle-length style dress Blanche always wore, and had the same body shape."

Billy nodded, his lips twisted to one corner in thought.

"What are you thinking?" I asked.

He sighed. "I thought the visions would have stopped by now."

"So, you think something is wrong with me?" I asked, feeling defensive, even though I knew it was unfair of me. He couldn't be expected to understand the truth when I had never fully explained it.

He shook his head forcefully. "No, of course I don't think that. It just means you have a bit further to go until you're fully recovered. I really wouldn't worry about it."

"But the vision did look remarkably similar to Blanche," I couldn't resist saying.

"It could be the same thing that happened when you saw Preacher Jacob," Billy said. "You saw an indistinct form, and then your memory filled it in later with the details of the person who passed away."

I wanted to point out that I had recognized the apparition as familiar the moment it appeared to me, not just after I heard it was Blanche Wilkins. But I wasn't ready to admit yet that the visions were real. If I did, I was afraid Billy would call up one of his doctor friends—the kind who wore white coats and carried big nets. And so, as I had done so many times before, I put off telling him.

"So, has Tucker been coming around to see you often?" Billy asked.

"Whoa, that was quite the change of topic," I teased, relieved nonetheless at the change of subject.

"Some would argue you changed the topic by bringing up the vision you saw in the field," he said. "I was just putting us back on course."

"Touché."

"You haven't answered the question," he said.

"No, Tucker hasn't been coming to the house. There's nothing going on between us, and there will continue to be nothing going on between us. I promise."

"Hey, it makes no difference to me either way," he said. "I was just curious."

"Yeah, sure," I teased. "The way you interrogated me for the answers seemed pretty laid back."

Even in the dim light of dusk, I could see Billy's cheeks were flushed. When he dropped me off, he jumped out of the driver's seat and ran around the truck to open my door.

"Sorry if I was a bit nosy," he said, staring down at his boots. "I've seen Tucker hit on a lot of women, and I'd hate for you to become another girl in a long string of disappointed women."

"Please," I said, hitting him playfully in the shoulder. "I am not a freshman girl swooning over the cutest senior in school. My tastes are much more refined now."

"Oh, really?" Billy asked. "Would you care to elaborate?"

I hit him in the shoulder again and then wrapped my arms around his neck for a hug. "Absolutely not. Goodnight, Billy."

He squeezed me back and then climbed into his truck with a wave. I watched him drive down the dirt road until his tail lights disappeared behind a line of trees. When I turned back towards the house, the smile I'd been sporting only moments before fell to disbelief. Standing next to the barn was the same figure I'd seen in the back field earlier in the day.

So close, it was obviously Blanche Wilkins. The apparition had a smoky kind of appearance, but I could make out the tightly permed hair, the broad flat nose, and the ring-covered fingers. It was unusual for a ghost to return to me again so soon after the first visit. Though, knowing what I did about Blanche, it wasn't surprising she would be the first to push the barriers. Blanche was demanding and not afraid to go after what she wanted—whether that was rent money or an egg roll from a tenant's Chinese takeout order.

"Blanche?" I called nervously, hoping my voice wasn't loud enough to draw the attention of anyone inside the house. They knew about me seeing spirits, but I wasn't ready to talk about this one just yet.

The bluish-white apparition wavered slightly. Was that a response?

"Why are you here?" I asked, taking a step forward.

Suddenly, the ghost Blanche froze up as if hit with a stun gun, seized, and disappeared.

5

After taking a few minutes to compose myself, I pushed open the door to the farmhouse. Except, it wouldn't open all the way. I pushed on the door again, and this time received a drowsy bleat in response.

"Hang on, there. Hold on a minute." I saw my grandpa walk by the crack in the door, groan as he picked something up, and then open the door for me. In his arms was a very sleepy Snowball. "This darned goat hasn't moved away from the front door since you left. She was depressed or something."

"Really? She usually goes up to my room as soon as the sun sets," I said, shrugging out of my jean jacket and hanging it from the hook behind the door.

"I gave her a bit of encouragement to get up the stairs a few times, but she wouldn't budge," Grandma said, a steaming mug of tea in front of her on the table.

"Does 'encouragement' mean a swift kick in the hind parts?" I asked.

My grandpa, usually stoic, bit back a laugh, and I knew I'd guessed correctly.

Grandma rolled her eyes and then pushed aside one of the kitchen chairs for me. "Come. Sit down. Tell me about your date."

"It was just dinner, Grandma. You were there when Billy asked."

"I know I was," she said, lips pressed into a thin line. "And it sounded like a date to me."

I sighed, knowing I wouldn't convince her otherwise. My grandma was anxious for me to get married so I could have children. She wanted there to be more little feet running through her house soon. She had always expected my parents to have more children for her to spoil, but they'd died in the car accident so young, leaving only me. And while I was technically a grandchild, she couldn't spoil me the way she'd planned. Instead, she'd had to raise me.

"What's that smell?" I asked, nose high in the air like a coon hound on the hunt.

"That is my award-winning pumpkin pie," Grandma said proudly.

I raised an eyebrow. "You've won awards for pumpkin pie?"

"No, but I will. And Margene Huffler will eat a big plate of humble pie."

"Grandma! You are diabolical," I said, wagging a finger at her, but unable to hide my smile.

"I sure hope so. I haven't even tasted it yet, though. It might not be any good." She stood up and pulled the pie out of the oven, setting it on a hot pad in the center of the table. The crust was golden brown, and the center was a gooey, rich orange. It looked delicious. "So, how was it?"

"How was what?" I asked, my mouth watering despite the fact I was stuffed from my burger and fries.

"Your date!"

"Not a date. But it was fine. Annie Colton is going to let me choose my own bridesmaid dress for her wedding, and we ran into Tucker at the diner. He may be dropping by soon for a visit."

"Good Heavens, we've had more male callers in the past few months than we did the entire time you were gone. You aren't running around breaking hearts, are ya?" Grandma looked up at me from beneath raised brows.

"When have I ever been known to run around breaking hearts?" I asked. "I never even had a boyfriend while I lived here."

"That's because you always had the boy next door hanging around," Grandma said, turning her attention back to her tea and quilting magazine. "No other boy stood a chance because Billy Stone never let you too far out of his sight."

I sighed and lifted myself out of the kitchen chair. "I'm off to bed."

"You sure you don't want some tea? If we stay up late gabbing long enough the pie will be cool, and we'll be able to have a late-night slice."

"Oh, leave the poor girl alone, Dorothy," Grandpa said from his spot on the couch. "She doesn't want to talk about her romantic life with her grandma."

Grandma shot the back of his head a dirty look. "I don't think it's that so much as you don't want to hear about it."

Before they could refocus too much of their energy back on me, I leaned forward and pecked my grandma on the cheek and then spun around to plant a kiss on the top of my grandpa's head. "Goodnight, you two."

"Sleep well, dear."

I was halfway up the stairs when I realized Snowball

wasn't following me, but was lying next to the couch, her furry chin on her hooves. "Are you coming, Snowball?"

She lifted her head, let out a dreary bleat, and then lowered it again.

"Guess not," I mumbled.

I took the rest of the stairs two at a time. A full day spent in the garden with Grandma and two sightings of a spirit in the same day was enough to completely wear me out. I needed a good night's sleep. When I reached the top of the stairs, I threw the door open and was a few steps into the room before I noted the temperature change. I stopped walking, a chill creeping up my neck. Then, I looked up and squealed.

The startled sound was out of me before I could draw it back in. It was a survival instinct, a reflex I couldn't control. There was a ghost standing in the middle of my bedroom. Well, floating, rather. Screaming seemed an appropriate response. Sure, this wasn't the first time I'd had a ghost in my room but it was the most unexpected.

Just as it had outside, the apparition flickered like a satellite television screen during a storm, seized up, and then flicked away in an instant.

As soon as the specter had disappeared, the rest of my senses kicked in again and I was able to hear the utter chaos happening on the first floor.

"My pie! Don't step on it, Ed!"

"Emma, are you all right? Snowball, get out of the way!"

Within the next ten seconds, my grandpa, grandma, and Snowball were all standing in the entrance to my bedroom, eyes wide, chests heaving. Snowball scurried between my grandparents' legs and, despite her reluctance to go upstairs with me just a few moments before, took a running leap onto my bed and huddled into the covers.

"Make yourself right at home, Snowball. Ruin my pie and then take a nap," Grandma muttered.

"Enough with the pie," Grandpa said, his voice unusually stern. "What is going on up here?"

They were all looking at me, waiting for an answer, and I said the first thing I could think of. "Spider."

There was a long pause, and then my grandma tilted her head to the side. "A spider?"

"You screamed like that because you saw a spider?" my grandpa asked, mouth hanging open in disbelief.

"Your goat hurled itself across the kitchen, knocked out the leg of my kitchen table, and ruined the pie I spent all evening making because you saw a spider?" Grandma asked, clearly trying to stack on the guilt.

"Sorry," I said, burying my head between my shoulders.

My grandpa shook his head one more time for good measure and then started down the stairs. "Girl has lost her country edge. Screamin' at a spider. She could wake the dead with shouting like that."

Grandma gave me a small, reluctant smile. "We'll spray for spiders tomorrow. Goodnight, dear."

"Goodnight, Grandma," I said. And then, shouting a bit louder so he'd hear me at the base of the stairs. "Goodnight, Grandpa."

He mumbled something and then I shut the door, pressing my back against it as I surveyed my room, checking to be sure I wouldn't be surprised by another ghost. Blanche was certainly persistent. I needed to figure out what she wanted from me, and fast. All I had to go on was that when ghosts appeared to me, it always seemed to involve foul play.

As soon as I felt confident I was alone again, except for Snowball who was curled up on the end of my bed, I pulled out my hotspot, fired up my laptop, and slipped under the covers. Blanche's son had only called me with the news of her death that day, but I was hoping there would be something online about her passing. Anything that would give me a clue as to her cause of death.

An internet search of her name brought up listings of the apartment units she had available and a few social media profiles, but there didn't seem to be anything regarding her death. Which meant it was either very recent or not worthy of note in any local papers.

Jay Wilkins had proven himself unhelpful on the phone. I had no reason to expect he'd take my call, and if he did, he'd likely hang up when he realized I was calling in regards to his mother's passing. And despite having lived in the New York City apartment for two years, I didn't feel comfortable calling a single one of my neighbors. I had never been known for being very outgoing, so we waved to one another when we passed in the halls, but that was it. Anyway, I couldn't live with Blanche Wilkins popping up unexpectedly forever. I needed to figure out what she wanted now.

One thing was for sure, if Blanche had come all the way from New York City to the middle of nowhere, Missouri, there had to be a good reason. And I intended to find out what it was.

6

I tossed and turned all night. Every time Snowball pressed her cold nose against my leg, I imagined it was a ghostly finger. Every flash of light from my computer charger or my phone charger or my alarm clock sent me shooting bolt upright in bed, prepared for another show from Blanche's persistent spirit. My lack of sleep gave me plenty of time to think, so by the time the sun was beginning to peek over the horizon, I knew what I had to do.

I had to go to New York.

The idea seemed crazy at first. I'd only been in Missouri a few months, and I was just beginning to find my footing again. In fact, I was starting to enjoy life away from the city more than I ever thought possible. However, the more I thought about going back to the city, the more it made sense. I would be able to ask around about Blanche, find out how she died and figure out why she kept showing up in my bedroom. Plus, I would have much better luck shopping for a bridesmaid dress in New York City than I would in Hillbilly Hollow, or even Branson, for that matter.

So, it was settled. I was going to go to New York, and there seemed to be no time like the present. I didn't want Blanche to become even more bold than she had been and suddenly appear in the laundry room while I was bathing in the old clawfooted tub, so I once again turned on my hot spot and began searching for flights to New York from Branson that same day.

My stomach began to growl as I spent the next thirty minutes searching for the best deal, finally booking a flight through National Airlines. Although I was still doing free-lance design work, it had certainly taken a backseat to farm work, and my budget was growing a little thin. I couldn't afford the luxury of extra leg room or priority boarding. My grandpa would have balked at even the suggestion of flying anything other than coach. In fact, he would have balked at the suggestion that he fly instead of drive his ancient, reliable farm truck halfway across the country. Maybe he was right and I had lost my country girl edge.

I had just finished plugging in my debit card information and confirming my flight for that afternoon when I heard tires rolling down the gravel driveway. I'd been up in my room later than I expected and it was already past seven, but it still seemed much too early for Grandpa to be leaving or for anyone else to be coming for a visit. I threw my hair into a messy bun, traded my flannel pajama pants for my trusty jeans, and threw a cream sweater on over my white night shirt. I made it downstairs just in time for my grandma to open the door and usher in Larry Tucker.

Once again, he was wearing street clothes instead of his sheriff's uniform, and he was holding a bouquet of white daisies.

"Good morning, Mrs. Hooper."

"Is everything all right?" Grandma asked, clearly concerned at the sight of the sheriff knocking on her door so early in the morning.

"Oh, yes, ma'am. I'm sorry. I didn't mean to scare ya. I'm here on personal business."

My stomach plummeted. Personal business? I thought it was supposed to be friends catching up.

"It's a bit early for personal business," Grandpa said, coming in the back door, a handful of fresh eggs from the coop bundled in his right hand.

Tucker looked up at the sound of Grandpa's voice and then noticed me standing at the bottom of the stairs. He held out the flowers towards me. "Hi, Emma."

I sighed and suddenly wished I'd taken more care to prepare myself for company. I still had morning breath and my face was always an oil slick before I washed it in the morning. "Good morning, Tucker."

"Sorry if I'm here too early. Guess I was a little eager for our date," he said.

Grandma spun around, mouth puckered into a tiny 'O' of surprise, but I was already shaking my head. "I'm sorry, we had a date?"

Tucker blinked a few times and lowered the bouquet. "I asked ya at the diner last night. You said I could come by the farmhouse whenever."

"I thought you meant to catch up." This was excruciatingly awkward, and I was regretting ever getting out of bed. If I'd still been in bed, my grandma likely would have sent him away. Or, she would have let him into my bedroom and this moment would have been even more uncomfortable than it already was.

"Well, yeah," he said, nodding slowly. "But I'd originally

come 'round to ask you on a date before I found out ya were already at the diner. So, when you told me I could come by the house anytime, I thought you meant I could come by anytime to ask you on a date."

Tucker was a good-looking man. Anyone with eyes could see that. The trouble was that he could walk down a straight hallway and get turned around. The man wasn't bright. How he had become a sheriff, the world might never know. What was more, he'd never shown any romantic interest in me before. Where was this even coming from?

"But I didn't know you wanted to ask me out," I said.

"But you said I could come by the farmhouse," he repeated.

I realized I could never fully explain to Tucker that I couldn't read his mind and therefore, when I'd told him he could come by for a visit, I hadn't understood what his intentions were. So, instead, I just nodded. "You're right, I did say that."

He smiled wide, showing me all of his pearly white teeth. "So, you ready to go, then?"

"Go where?" I asked.

"On our date," he said, holding up the flowers to me again. "I have a picnic packed in the cooler. I figured we'd go down to the river and do some fishin'."

My grandma was pressed against the wall, trying to make herself as small as possible while still ogling the encounter before her. She was snapping her head back and forth between me and Tucker like she was watching a tennis match.

"I'm so sorry, Tucker, but I can't today. I'm busy."

His brows pulled together. "But you said I could come by the house today."

"I know I did, but I completely forgot that I'm going out of town today. It's a last minute trip," I said, deciding to lie about having pre-planned the trip, rather than explain to him why I'd booked a flight that morning when he had so clearly and obviously asked me out on a date the night before.

"Out of town?" Grandma asked, unable to remain a quiet observer. "Where are you going?"

"New York. I have a few things I need to take care of and I'd like to do it before winter arrives. I don't want to be flying in a snowstorm." Again, skimming over the truth seemed to be my best option.

"I didn't know you were leaving," Grandma said.

"Sorry." I winced. "I should have told you sooner. I hope it doesn't ruin any plans?"

She shook her head. "No, it just seems so sudden. We just got you back a few months ago."

"It's only for a few days," I assured her. "I'll be here again before you know it."

"Well, that settles it then," Tucker said, clapping his hands together.

Somehow, I had completely forgotten Tucker was standing in the doorway. I turned to him, head tilted to the side. "Settles what?"

"I've always wanted to see New York in the fall, and I've got a lot of unused vacation time. This is perfect." Tucker was beaming at me, but I was just squinting back at him, trying to make sense of what he was saying. "When does your flight leave? I probably can't get a seat on the same flight, but I bet I can work it out so we arrive in New York around the same time. My dad has a lot of frequent flier miles he can loan me."

The reality of his words began to sink in, and the urge to both laugh and cry overwhelmed me. "Tucker, are you saying you're going to come with me?"

He nodded. "Yep! Like I said, I've always wanted to see New York, and what better way to see it than with a true-blue New Yorker?"

I just shook my head, unable to think of a polite way to explain to him how much I didn't want him to accompany me.

"That sounds like a great idea," Grandpa said from the kitchen. He was cracking eggs into a large mixing bowl for scrambled eggs. "I never liked the idea of you running around that city by yourself, Emma. Now, you'll have someone to look out for you."

"I lived there for years without any problems, Grandpa," I said, glaring at the back of his head.

"Didn't you say just yesterday that your landlady was murdered?" Grandma asked.

"No, I'm not sure how she died," I said exasperated.

"All the more reason to take Tucker with you," Grandpa said.

Tucker grinned cheerfully. "Sure enough. I'll be your bodyguard in the big city, Emma. I don't have jurisdiction there, but I've been trained in hand-to-hand combat. Keepin' you safe won't be a problem."

"There won't be any need for any kind of combat. And really, Tucker, I'll be fine. I can go alone."

"I know ya can, but now ya don't have to," he said.

"Then, it's settled," my grandpa said, whisking his eggs, still having never turned around once.

"Then, it's settled," Tucker repeated.

I looked at my grandma, putting as much emotion into

my eyes as possible, hoping she would help dig me out of this hole. Instead, she smiled at me, a wide, mischievous smile, and clapped her hands once in front of her, interlacing her fingers. "It's settled."

Her words were the last nail in the coffin. I was going to New York City with Larry Tucker. It was settled.

7

BILLY: When were U planning 2 tell me U and Tucker skipped from dating 2 taking trips together?

I READ Billy's text and groaned. I didn't know why I thought it would be possible to get through the trip to New York City without anyone finding out Tucker was tagging along. In Hillbilly Hollow, it was hard to keep what you ate for dinner a secret. The gossip network in the town was well-refined and efficient. I had barely managed to finish packing my suitcase before he'd found out the news.

ME: I was waiting 2 tell U at me and Tucker's wedding. I'm thinking orange and purple for the colors.

BILLY: That's so not funny. Seriously, what's up?

ME: I have 2 go 2 NYC to take care of some things and Tucker invited himself. My grandparents encouraged it. Blame them.

I WAS STARING at my phone, waiting for Billy's response when my phone began to ring. It was Billy.

He started talking before I could even say hello. "Do you need me to talk to him for you? Because you shouldn't have to go with him if it makes you uncomfortable. I can tell him to back off."

Where was this protective side of Billy coming from? He used to splash me with ditch water and run ahead to try and leave me in the woods when we were kids, but now he was my bodyguard?

"It's fine, really. He'll have his own hotel room and he hasn't been to the city before, so he'll be busy sight-seeing. I doubt we'll even see each other all that much."

There was a long pause on the other end of the phone. "Why did your grandparents encourage it? Do they like him or something?"

"I don't think there's anyone who doesn't like Tucker," I said with a nervous laugh.

He hummed. "Yeah, I guess so."

"Besides, their problem was me going to the city alone. They just want someone there to look out for me."

"You lived in New York for years by yourself," he said.

"I know but try explaining that to them. They're stubborn, and this was the easiest way to pacify them."

"I could go." His voice was low, more of a mumble than anything else.

"Go where?" I asked, knowing what he meant, but still not able to believe what he was offering.

"To New York," he said. "I could go with you if you needed someone to accompany you. I haven't been to New York, either."

"Could you leave your practice so suddenly? My flight leaves this afternoon." The thought of Billy and Tucker following me around New York popped into my head, and a sudden dread filled my stomach.

"I guess not," he said, voice trailing off.

"It will only be a few days. Don't worry, Billy."

"I'm not worried."

"Good," I said. There were a few beats of silence. "Maybe when I get back we can grab dinner at the diner."

"Yeah, definitely. Or somewhere else, too. There's a good Italian place in Branson that just opened up. And a drive-in theater not too far."

Dinner and a drive-in movie? It would be hard to convince Suzy and my grandma that wasn't a date.

"Yeah, that would be great," I said.

"Great," Billy said, sounding much more cheerful than he had when he'd called. "Then, I guess I'll talk to you in a few days."

"I'll call you when I'm back in town."

As soon as I hung up, I pocketed my phone, grabbed my suitcase, and lugged it downstairs. I tossed it into the back of the old farm truck, kissed my grandparents goodbye, and promised them I'd be home in a few days. Then, the ancient engine roared to life and I was off.

8

———————

Somehow Tucker managed to book a seat on my flight from Branson to New York City. So, even though I made it to the airport and through security without running into him, he found me while I was waiting at the gate to board.

"Which seat are ya in?" he asked, holding up his ticket. I leaned over and read his: 16C.

I held in a groan. "16A."

"Great. I bet we can get 16B to swap with one of us, so we can sit next to each other."

And Tucker was right. 16B was a man in a business suit who didn't seem to care about much outside of his laptop, and he was more than willing to switch seats with Tucker. I spent the entire flight pressed against the window, pretending to sleep. It was going to be a long trip.

When we landed, Tucker immediately began his sightseeing tour. He craned his neck to look through every window we passed, oftentimes holding up the flow of passengers trying to make their way through the airport.

"Do you have any place to stay yet?" I asked.

He looked at me, eyebrows pulled together. "I haven't booked anything. Do ya have a guest room at your place?"

I shook my head. "No, it's a one-bedroom. Two-bedrooms in New York are too expensive for my budget."

I didn't admit that I had briefly had a roommate at one point and that I did, in fact, still have that previous roommate's old futon in the living room, where Tucker could have slept. It seemed better not to encourage him.

He nodded, looking disappointed. "Okay. So, I'll just get a hotel close to your apartment. No problem."

"There's a hospitality desk over there." A woman with bright red hair and a nametag reading 'Deanna' stood behind the desk. She looked Tucker up and down and smiled.

He turned back to me, eyes wide. "Can't you help me find one?"

"Deanna will make everything so much easier. Trust me. She'll get you set up with a nice place and a good nightly rate. You get your living situation sorted out and then we'll meet back up later."

"You're leavin' me here?"

"I have some things I need to sort out at my apartment that would be boring for you."

"I don't mind," Tucker said hopefully.

I waved him away. "You'll be fine. Just get a hotel, snag a taxi out front, and call me when you're ready. You have my number, right?"

He nodded.

"Great. Then, it's a plan?"

Tucker looked at Deanna and then back at me, obviously conflicted. Finally, he shrugged, nodded, and walked towards the desk. Deanna visibly brightened at her luck. I was sure Tucker was one of the most handsome travelers she'd talk to all day. Maybe even all week.

As soon as Tucker was involved in conversation with the very flirty Deanna, I rolled my suitcase out front and waved down a taxi. I felt bad ditching Tucker at the airport when he so clearly wanted to stick together, but I hadn't been to my apartment in a few months. And for some reason, I wanted to be alone when I went back.

A cab pulled up in front of me, and I began moving towards it, bending forward to look through the window and wave at the driver. He had dark hair and a thick beard, and he lifted his hand to wave back. Except, as soon as he got a good look at me, he froze. His eyes widened, and before I could even contemplate what was happening, he drove away.

I watched him speed out of the airport pick-up zone without a passenger, and I couldn't understand. In all my years in New York City, I'd never seen any cabbie willingly drive away without a passenger in his car while on duty. Every mile they drove with an empty car was a mile they weren't getting paid for. Why wouldn't he want my money?

Another cab replaced that one and the driver—an Indian man with a big smile—popped the trunk for my luggage before I could even ask. He seemed to have no trouble at all taking me on as a passenger, and by the time we reached my apartment, I'd forgotten about the first driver all together.

My apartment building was a narrow six-story walkup with a set of stairs running along the right side and apartments stacked on top of one another on the left. There were three units per floor, except for the basement which had been converted into one large unit for Blanche's son, Jay.

I slid my key into the door, and it felt routine, as if I'd

never left. The door clicked open, and I stepped into the yellow and green-tiled lobby. A wall of metal mailboxes was off to the right, and I pulled out my mail key to check mine. As soon as the small door opened, envelopes and coupons began spilling out onto the floor. I'd set up a forwarding address at my grandparents' house in Missouri, but clearly some people didn't get the message. I shoved bundles of mail into my purse, content to sort through it later.

"As I live and breathe."

The voice startled me for a moment, but then I recognized who it was. When I turned around, I was wearing a warm smile. "Mable, how have you been?"

"Still alive," she said with a laugh, and then she sobered. "I suppose I shouldn't say that considering the news around here these days. Did you hear about Blanche?"

I nodded. "I heard. How sad. Do they have any idea how it happened?"

She pulled her thin shoulders into a shrug. "No one tells me anything, and I don't get out as much as I used to."

That was an understatement of epic proportions. Mable Abernathy had lived in the same apartment for twenty years, and to my knowledge, she hadn't left in that long, either. No one had ever seen her leave the building, she had her groceries and medications delivered to her door, and with the invention of the internet, her life of solitude had become even easier. Of course, it wasn't total solitude. She would stand in the doorway of her apartment to see who came and went from the building, popping out every time someone she recognized passed by, so they could chat.

I said, "I haven't heard anything, either."

"If you do, you'll let me know?" she asked, her pale face pulled up hopefully, drawn in eyebrows stretched towards her hairline.

"Of course. I'll only be back for a few days, but I'll be sure to knock and see you again before I leave."

"You better. Oh, and before you leave, let me grab you something." She disappeared from the door for a few seconds, and I heard movement inside her apartment. Then, she reappeared with a paper plate full of brownies. "Please take some of these sweets off my hands. I'll eat too many of them if they're around."

"Oh, I've certainly missed you, Mable," I said, patting my stomach. "No one makes a brownie like you."

"I'm a humble woman, but even I have to agree with you there." She winked at me and then clicked her door closed, bolting it immediately.

With my luggage and newly acquired brownies in tow, I walked up the three flights of stairs to my apartment. The door was a bit tight at first, swollen from humidity and lack of use, but I managed to kick it open. The room smelled musty as soon as I walked in, which I initially attributed to the lack of airflow, but as I dropped Mable's brownies on the counter and stepped into the space, I realized my rug was damp.

My shoe squished in the rug, water leeching out of it and spread out across the wood floor.

"What in the—?" I mumbled, my mouth hanging open. I followed a trail of wetness from the edge of the rug all the way to the window, and then I solved the problem. The window had been leaking.

I sighed. How had I forgotten about my leaky window? It had caused havoc for me all Spring the year before, and no matter how many times Blanche sent the maintenance guy in to fix it, the next time it rained, the window would leak all over my carpet. I'd gotten pretty good at strategically placing towels and cups around the frame and on the floor to catch the water, but considering I hadn't been home in months, the water had soaked through the towels, filled the cups, and spread across half of my living room. Luckily, my furniture was safe, and my books were all in a shelf in the bedroom, but my rug was a goner. It smelled like mildew and some of the colors had begun to bleed due to the constant damp.

I set to work cleaning the mess. I moved my coffee table, sofa, and armchair to the edges of the room and rolled the damp rug. As it folded in on itself, water began to leak from the ends like a Swiss Roll with too much cream. I ran to the pantry and grabbed two trash bags to tie around the ends and collect some of the water so I didn't leave a stream of water all the way through the apartment building. Ten minutes later, I was heaving my sopping wet rug—which looked like a damp q-tip thanks to the sagging trash bags on either end—down three flights of stairs and to the dumpster in the alley. The sight of the beautiful rug I'd bought on clearance just a year before in the dumpster was sad.

There's $150 down the drain.

I hoofed it back up the stairs, pulled out my mop and bucket, and began the arduous process of cleaning my wood laminate floors. By the time I finished, my back was aching from bending forward, my arms hurt from the repetitive movement of squeezing water out of the mop, and my forehead was sweaty. But my apartment smelled slightly less damp, and rug or no rug, it looked nice. Cozy.

I was tempted to sit down on the couch and kick my feet up, but I knew if I did, I'd never stand up again. So, despite my protesting feet, I dabbed the sweat from my face, picked up the brownies from the counter, and headed down to the basement. Jay Wilkins and I needed to have a discussion.

9

My apartment building was surprisingly affordable, but it lacked many of the amenities of nearby spaces. No resident gym, no washers and dryers, and a general lack of pleasant aesthetics. The apartment units had all been painted a neutral white, but the hallways hadn't been updated since the 1980s, at least. The color scheme alone—varying shades of green, yellow, and brown—made that abundantly clear. But the yellow glass votives and shaggy orange carpet runners finished the deal. The building was ugly.

The basement, however, belonged to Jay Wilkins, and he apparently had been given the option to renovate. As soon as I opened the door to the basement, I felt as if I'd stepped into a villain's lair. The floors were a shiny slate gray, and the walls were a dark charcoal color with light fixtures shining bright white beams from the ceiling to the floor every few feet.

Prior to the renovation, there had been three units in the basement, but now two of the doors had been sheet rocked over, leaving one door at the far end of the hall. The door was the same dark wood as the floor. I stood in front of it, Mable's brownies held in front of me as an offering, and pressed the small illuminated door bell next to the door. I heard a low gong-like sound echo through the apartment, followed by a deep voice.

"I'm coming." It was a grumble more than anything else.

When the door opened, Jay Wilkins stood before me in all his glory, looking exactly as I'd pictured him. Balding, with red hair, round middle, and wearing a grungy rock t-shirt. It was also apparent by the raise of his eyebrows that he had no idea who I was.

"Emma Hooper," I said, extending the brownies. "We talked on the phone."

He grabbed the brownies but didn't lose his look of suspicion. "I thought you were out of town."

"I had to come back to take care of a few things, and I thought I'd stop by to offer my condolences."

He hummed in understanding. "Well, thanks."

The door was halfway shut when I shoved my foot against it, stopping it from slamming in my face. "I also came because I have a problem."

"That makes more sense." He rolled his eyes. "What's wrong?"

Clearly, our tenant/landlord relationship was off to a great start.

"I've had trouble in the past with my window leaking. Maintenance was sent in several different times to fix it, but it still leaks every time it rains. I actually just had to throw out an expensive rug because there was a lot of water damage during the months I was gone."

"You'll have to take that up with your renter's insurance," he said, wagging a finger at me. "I'll send Paul up to look at the window this next week."

Paul had already been in my apartment four different times, caulking every crevice he could find, and it had done nothing. But I had a strong suspicion I would have to bring a lot more than brownies to convince Jay that he needed to hire a professional to replace the window.

"I'm only in town for a few days before I have to leave again."

He sighed. "I'll have to look at Paul's schedule and get back to you. I'll call you."

Once again, he tried to slam the door.

"Is there any way we could schedule it now? I'm sure you're very busy, and I'd hate for you to forget and then come back to another flooded apartment."

He stared at me for a long time, looking like he was trying to make me disappear with his mind, before stepping aside and letting me into his apartment. I smiled and walked past him.

Much like the hallway, the interior was decorated mostly in shades of gray and black with sci-fi movie posters and death metal rock band album covers hung all over the walls. It looked like a slightly weird kid's college dorm room. But it was massive. The entire apartment was open concept with an all stainless-steel kitchen running along the back wall and a dining room/living room/gaming room taking up the rest of the space.

A room that appeared to have once been a bathroom for one of the units had been renovated into an office space. Jay flipped on the light switch and turned on the computer monitor in the room. In a matter of a few clicks, he pulled up a chart.

"Paul is free tomorrow at two in the afternoon. Otherwise, he has a slot next week," he said in a glum voice.

"Tomorrow at two it is."

"Which apartment number?" he asked.

"3B."

"What was your name again?"

"Emma Hooper," I said, feeling strange about being in Jay's apartment when he didn't even remember my name.

When he finished, he stood up and immediately moved back towards the front door, evidently eager to have me out of his apartment as quickly as possible.

"This is a nice place you have down here," I said, looking around. Aside from his choice of décor, it really would be an incredible apartment. One the same size would cost a fortune in rent. "Hopefully your mom gave you a discount."

He grimaced at my joke. "She made sure I paid, believe me."

It was clear Jay Wilkins didn't have a good relationship with his mother, and it was also clear that he was on the verge of forcefully pushing me from his apartment. I was running out of time to start a conversation and casually bring up her death, so I decided to go for it. Like ripping off a bandage.

"Do you know how she died?" I asked.

He shrugged and looked down at the floor. "They have to do an autopsy first. One EMT suspected foul play."

"Murder, you mean?"

"That's my understanding of 'foul play,'" he said sarcastically. "But I doubt it. I'm not sure what happened. Another EMT guessed she was done in by a heart attack. I told him she'd have to have one for that to be true. I don't think he got the joke."

I chuckled to make him feel better, though I also failed to see how the joke could be construed as funny. Most people, when faced with their mother's dead body, wouldn't make jokes about how horrible she was.

"She did seem a little cold," I admitted cautiously, unsure whether this was the kind of situation where only he could say bad things about his mom, or whether her character was open for public comment.

For the first time, he laughed. "A little? The woman was Antarctica. She offered me this apartment as a gift, but the moment my house sold, she began holding it over my head. She told me that I'd be nothing without her, that she was the only woman who could ever care about me."

I tried to hide my shock, but I worried it was spread all across my face. I hadn't expected him to be so candid with me, or for Blanche to be quite so cruel.

"Not that she would know," Jay said, rolling his eyes. "She demanded I eat dinner with her five nights a week, usually both weekend evenings. So, even if I got a date, I couldn't take her to dinner or my mom would've had me evicted."

"She threatened to evict me once, too," I said. "I had to prop the front door open with my shoe while I was carrying in a new chair and she told me I'd be kicked out if I ever did anything like that again."

He shook his head. "Yeah, Mom was always power hungry. She took advantage of it wherever she could. She would cut the power to my apartment if she thought I was playing too many video games."

I nodded sympathetically, though based on the collection of energy drinks and fast food containers lying around his gaming computer, I had to wonder whether Blanche hadn't been on to something there. I, of course, didn't say this.

"She wanted to evict an elderly resident, so she could make more money. She would rave on and on about rent control, and how much money she was losing every month because of it. I understand the importance of turning a profit but turning out little old ladies is beyond even me."

"Do you mean Mable Abernathy?" I asked.

He shrugged. "I'm not good with names."

"The woman who lives on the first floor right by the front door?"

"I don't know," he said, a bit more firmly this time. "I never brought the topic up with Mom willingly and I didn't like to egg her on when she got worked up about it. It doesn't matter now, anyway."

Except, maybe it did? If Blanche was seriously going to try and evict someone, then she could have placed a target on her own back. I had to admit that the idea of Mable Abernathy killing anyone—especially since she hadn't left her apartment in twenty years—was absurd. But I also wanted to pursue every opportunity.

I was about to ask Jay if there was anyone else in the building who may have been upset with his mother, but a knock at his door interrupted me.

"Someone else?" he asked, obviously surprised. Apparently, he didn't get many guests.

As he was walking to the door, the person knocked again and then rang the doorbell.

"I'm coming," he barked.

"Good afternoon. Sheriff Larry Tucker here. Is Emma Hooper around?"

I winced. Even if he hadn't offered his full name—title and all—I'd recognize that lazy drawl anywhere.

"Okay, what's going on?" Jay asked, throwing the door wide and stepping back, trying to separate himself from the situation. He looked back at me. "Are you in trouble with the law or something?"

"No, no. Not Emma," Tucker said with a laugh. "I'm just

a friend. The lady in the first-floor apartment told me she saw Emma come down here a few minutes ago."

Mable Abernathy sure had a sharp awareness of her surroundings for being as old as she was.

Jay crossed his arms over his chest. "Okay, well you two can have your reunion upstairs. My house isn't a meeting place."

An odd look crossed Tucker's face, but he looked mostly confused rather than offended. "Are you ready to go, Emma?"

In fact, no, I wasn't. I had quite a few more questions for Jay, but it was obvious he wasn't going to be answering any more of them now that Tucker had made a surprise appearance. If I wanted to talk to Jay again, I'd have to come armed with a lot more than brownies.

"Sure," I said, trying to hide my disappointment.

Tucker smiled and turned sideways to let me pass through the door. He gave a hearty wave to Jay, who frowned and then slammed the door closed.

"This hallway makes a real decorative statement, don't it?" Tucker asked, looking around at the lights and the dark gray walls. "Does your apartment look like this?"

"No, it doesn't." I wondered whether the question hadn't been Tucker's attempt at asking if we could go up to my apartment but based on the easy smile still on his face, I doubted it.

"Are you as hungry as me? Those peanuts on the plane didn't last me long," Tucker said.

I had to admit I was starving. The physical activity of cleaning up my flooded apartment paired with the amateur sleuthing had really worked up an appetite.

"I could definitely eat," I said.

"We could stay in or go out," Tucker said.

I thought about my pantry upstairs, and how it was stocked with nothing more than a few cans of soup and a bag of mold that had once been bread.

"If we want to eat anything even halfway edible, we should probably go out. My pantry is in a pretty sad state after all these months away."

Tucker held the front door of the apartment open for me and I squeezed past him. Before I could even touch the first step, he grabbed my shoulder and pulled me back.

"Whoa, watch out," he said. "There's a dead bird there."

I looked down and there was a gray and black pigeon lying on the front step. It looked perfectly healthy except for the fact it wasn't breathing.

"Ew. Gross. That wasn't here half an hour ago when I walked through," I said.

"Or when I just came in," Tucker said, looking around. "Weird."

It was strange that the bird had chosen the stairs of my building to die on, but stranger things had certainly happened. I walked around the bird and down to the sidewalk.

"Even after seein' a dead bird, I'm still starving," Tucker said. Then, he clapped his hands together excitedly. "Okay, New Yorker. Show me your city!"

Tucker was definitely going to be one of those enthusiastic tourists who marveled at the urine-soaked subway system and took pictures of every skyscraper he saw, but I couldn't help but find his excitement a little contagious.

I said, "Okay. First stop: pizza."

10

There were always too many amazing pizza places in New York City to count. There was a shop on every block, and everyone claimed to have the best slice around. I made it my mission when I first moved to the city to find the best pizza, but after three weeks of eating nothing but pizza, everything began to taste the same, so I opted for convenience. And nothing was more convenient than Matteo's.

"You have a pizza shop that's walking distance from your apartment," Tucker said, putting his hands on his hips and looking back and forth from my apartment building to the little corner shop in front of us.

I nodded. "Isn't it great?"

Matteo's sat in a glass-fronted shop with a faded green overhang above the door. The inside of the restaurant was microscopic, with only enough room for two tables and four chairs. Occasionally, someone would come in and sit down at a table to eat, but Matteo would usually rush them out after a few minutes. He didn't like when people lingered in the store. *Don't you have a table at home?*

The shop was warm, and the windows were steamed up because of the chill outside.

"Haven't seen you in a while," Matteo said when I walked in. The flat line of his mouth gave no indication of whether he thought my absence was a good thing or a bad thing.

"I've been out of town."

He nodded. "What can I get you?"

"Two pepperonis," I said.

He nodded again and turned around to grab our slices from the still-steaming pepperoni pizza sitting behind him. He put each on a stack of two paper plates for added strength, and then tossed them up on the counter.

"Nice place you got here," Tucker said when he handed over his debit card.

Matteo raised an eyebrow at him.

"The pizza looks delicious," he continued, despite how clear it was Matteo didn't want to engage.

I'd always liked New York because of the lack of small talk. Most people were content to simply provide a service and go along with their day. Whereas, I couldn't pay for my items at the grocery store in Hillbilly Hollow without learning about the checker's grandmother's failed hip replacement and the details of the ensuing law suit.

Matteo handed back the card and disappeared into the kitchen without a word. Tucker, to his credit, still didn't seem fazed.

"This looks great." He grabbed the crust and began to lift it straight up, causing his toppings to slide down towards the tip.

"Whoa, hold on." I pulled the pizza out of his hands. "You have to fold the crust for more stability, otherwise you'll lose your toppings."

I demonstrated, and then Tucker followed suit. He groaned after his first bite. "Okay, this is the best pizza I've ever had."

The bell above the front door rang as we walked back onto the street, pizza in hand. We ate and walked, and I pointed out the bodegas on the corners stocked with everything from candy to cigarettes and cold cuts. Tucker was amazed at the sheer amount of different ethnic grocery stores available to buy from.

I tossed my empty paper plate into the trash and pulled out my phone to check the time, when I noticed I had a few text messages. I had three from Suzy over the last two hours.

SUZY: R U in NYC yet? Is Tucker really with you?

SUZY: Srsly. U need to talk to Billy. He's being crazy.

SUZY: At this point, Billy thinks U and Tucker are eloping. Call him.

WHAT WAS SHE TALKING ABOUT? I'd already talked to Billy. He knew everything was fine. I shook my head and checked the rest of my notifications. I had SEVEN messages from Billy.

BILLY: Let me know when your flight lands.

BILLY: I mean, U don't have 2. But I'd like 2 know U made it safely.

BILLY: U haven't texted back, but I'm going 2 assume U made it safely.

BILLY: Send pictures of your New York apartment. Suzy and I want 2 see where U live.

BILLY: Or should I ask Tucker 2 send pics? Maybe he'd actually answer his phone. LOL.

BILLY: I ordered cheese fries at the diner. I'll wrap up the leftovers and save them for when U return...if U return.

BILLY: Just kidding. I ate them.

"EVERYTHING OKAY?" Tucker asked.

I looked up and noticed him looking over my shoulder at my screen. I quickly locked the phone and shoved it back in my pocket.

"Yeah, totally fine. Just some friends checking to make sure I made it here alright."

"Ya mean Billy?" Tucker asked, a hint of animosity in his voice.

"And Suzy," I added.

"So, Billy has always been just a friend?" Tucker asked, balling up his paper plate in his hands and dunking it into a trash can as we passed.

"We've been friends since we were kids, if that's what you mean."

"Never anything more than that?" he asked. "You two never dated?"

A startled laugh burst out of me. "No. Billy and me? No. Never."

"Just checkin'," he said, wrapping an arm around my shoulders. "I wouldn't want to step on any toes. It's good for the Sheriff to keep friendly with everyone."

My eyes felt like they were bulging out of my head. Larry Tucker had his arm around my shoulders. He was hitting on me. What was I supposed to do?

I laughed nervously and stepped away from him, bending down to pick up a random piece of trash off the sidewalk and drop it into a nearby dumpster. Apparently, littering was a very big deal for me now.

So many women back in Hillbilly Hollow would be screaming at me right now. Tucker was a hot commodity, which made it even more strange that he had set his sights on me. It wasn't that I wasn't a good-looking person, but I was one of the few women who had never once tried to throw myself at him. I had never encouraged him in any way, so why had he gone to such lengths to try and spend time with me? He'd crossed the country for a date.

Tucker caught up to me and placed his arm around my shoulders again, not at all discouraged by my subtle attempt to shake him off. "What should we do now? We could go dancin'. I'm sure the clubs in New York are a lot different than the country clubs back home."

"I've never really been much for going to clubs," I said. "I don't drink or dance much."

"Oh," he said, sounding only slightly disappointed. "Well, then what's there to do on a Sunday night in the city?"

I was about to make the excuse that I was tired and suggest we each head to our respective beds for the night when someone on the opposite side of the street caught my eye. Unlike the passersby who had hoods pulled up and earbuds in, steadily moving toward their destinations, this person was standing perfectly still and looking towards me. It took me less than a second to realize why.

It was Blanche. She'd shown herself to me three times in one day in Hillbilly Hollow, but I hadn't seen her since arriving in New York, which seemed strange, especially since I had been in the building where she died. But here she was, finally, appearing to me in the middle of the sidewalk.

I stopped moving and turned towards her. She had on the same ankle-length dress and the same gaudy jewelry as the last time I'd seen her, but this time her mouth seemed to be moving. I squinted, trying to get a better look at her silvery form. Was she saying something? Trying to give me a message?

"Emma?" Tucker asked behind me, but I ignored him and stepped towards the curb.

I needed to get a better look at Blanche's spirit. I needed to know what she was saying. It could be a clue, and considering how far I was from solving this crime, I needed all the help I could get.

"Emma, where are you going?" Tucker asked, his voice fading into the background, joining the din of the city. I'd forgotten how loud the city could be. Waking up in my old attic room at Grandma's and Grandpa's, the only noise I heard was the rooster and the shuffle of hooves from the barn out back. It was a peaceful kind of noise. But here it was distant horns and city buses and music coming from open windows and bars. I wished it was quieter so I could hear Blanche.

Blanche's lips continued moving, but as I got closer, I still couldn't hear anything. Suddenly, her mouth stopped moving and her eyes grew wide. Funnily enough, she looked like she was seeing a ghost. Her entire body seized up, shaking for a moment before she winked away and disappeared.

I took a few more steps towards her, hand extended as if to grab her, hold her to this world. But it was already too late. She was gone.

"Emma!"

Tucker's cry was too loud for me to ignore that time, and just as I turned to look back at him, I saw a flash of lights next to me. For a second, I thought it was another apparition, this one barreling towards me like it hoped to run me over, but then I heard the horn.

"Get out of the road, lady!" A cab driver had his head sticking out of a window and was shaking his fist at me.

I felt hands on my shoulders and then Tucker was yanking me back to the curb. "What are you doing? You were almost killed."

Almost killed. Again. It was the second time I'd almost been crushed by a taxi. I closed my eyes, trying to steady my heartbeat, and I saw the taxi. Only, it wasn't the same taxi. This one was older, banged up around the bumper and chipping paint around the grill. Also, it was daytime instead of late in the evening. I was using the crosswalk, and then the day was shattered by a shrill horn and the squeal of tires. I looked over just in time to catch a glimpse of the bearded man behind the wheel, eyes wide, and his nametag hanging from the rearview mirror: Ernest. Then, the cab hit me.

I opened my eyes, gasping for breath. I hadn't been breathing.

"Are ya hurt?" Tucker asked, dragging me up the curb and shaking my shoulders. "What's wrong? Your face looks blue."

I blinked a few times, trying to clear my head. I'd just seen the man responsible for my ghostly visions. The man who had hit me all those months ago and fled the scene. The same man I'd seen in a taxi at the airport earlier today. That explained why he had driven away so wildly. Because although I hadn't recognized him, he had recognized me, and he didn't want to get caught for his crime.

"I'm okay. I just can't believe I was almost hit by a car," I said, making up the most plausible excuse for my behavior.

"I've lived here long enough that I should know better than to walk out in the street."

"Why were you in the road?" he asked.

"I...I thought I recognized someone."

Tucker frowned and looked across the road, which was empty now. Then he turned back to me and nodded. "Let's get you home, okay? It's been a long day."

"Okay," I agreed.

I was still shaken up, but my fear was quickly being harnessed into something else: determination. I was going to find that cab driver again. And this time, he wouldn't get away.

11

I f there was one thing New York City had over Hillbilly Hollow, it was that my mattress in my apartment was worlds more comfortable than the one I'd bought at the mattress shop in Missouri. The main difference was that this one was broken in. It had a small crater in the center where I lay, which I knew probably meant I needed to replace it, but it felt like crawling into a person-sized nest.

Perhaps Tucker was right, and the full day of travel had exhausted me, or maybe it was just a coincidence. But I slept more solidly than I had in weeks. It was an uninterrupted eight hours of sleep. I didn't think I even rolled over. When I woke up in the morning, my body felt stiff from lying in the same position all night but rested.

My pantry was still in desperate need of stocking, so I threw on a baseball hat and my leggings and walked down to the bakery a few blocks over. I couldn't be back in the city and not indulge in a fresh baked bagel with cream cheese, and a steaming cup of black coffee.

While I walked back to the apartment, I made the split

second decision to call Billy. It was a Monday morning, so I assumed he would be busy at work and I'd get his machine. But he picked up on the second ring.

"Hey Emma," he said, his tone sounding surprised to hear from me.

"Hey Billy. What's going on?"

"I'm at work, but between patients at the moment. What are you guys doing?"

I knew Billy thought he was being clever by asking how *we* were doing, but I could see right through it.

"Well, *I*, singular, am just walking back to my apartment. I went out for a bagel and some coffee—by myself."

"Why are you talking like that?" he asked, trying to sound confused.

I laughed. "You are ridiculous, Billy. Do you think I want to be here with Tucker?"

"Your private life is your business," he said.

"Right now I'm making it your business, too. I'd rather be here alone, but Tucker invited himself. And I didn't message you back yesterday because I walked in to a flooded apartment that I had to clean and then I was almost hit by a car last night."

He gasped. "What? Are you okay?"

"Almost," I repeated. "I'm fine. It has just been a crazy twenty-four hours. But I wanted to call and let you know that I made it to New York safely, and the plan is still to be home in a few days."

"I'm glad you're okay," he said, sounding genuine. Then, his tone became much snarkier. "Do the two of you have a lot of sight-seeing scheduled?"

"Oh, yes," I said dramatically. "I think Tucker will love helping me track down the man who hit me with his taxi a few months ago and then fled the scene. It will be a day for the scrapbook."

"I thought you didn't know who hit you?"

"I didn't, and I guess I still don't, but I saw him yesterday. He was parked outside of the airport and he drove away before I could talk to him, but I have a name. Ernest."

"What are the chances of that? Like, 1 in 500,000?" he asked. "Are you sure it was him?"

"I know it sounds unbelievable, but I'm positive." And I was. Absolutely.

There was a long pause. "Are you sure it's a good idea to go tracking him down, Emma? I mean, he hit you with his car and ran away? That doesn't suggest he's a great guy. What if he's dangerous?"

"Tucker will be with me."

Billy groaned. "That doesn't make me feel better. Besides, he's off duty and powerless there. Anyway, how many different cab companies are there in New York? How are you going to find this guy?"

I'd been thinking about that all morning and hadn't come up with a solid solution yet. "I don't know. The names of these cab drivers have to be in a database somewhere, right? Maybe I could pay someone to find it for me."

"Like a hacker?" Billy asked, sounding, if possible, even more skeptical.

Suddenly, I had a flash of memory. When I'd once had trouble logging into the tenant portal of the apartment building's new website, Blanche had told me she would need to go talk to the 'computer wizard' she'd hired to make it for her.

He lives right here in the building, which is convenient, but he did so much fancy stuff that I couldn't keep up. I'll pass your complaint along and have him take a look at it.

Maybe her computer wizard would be able to work his magic for me.

I jogged up the steps, held my coffee between my side and elbow, and punched in my code for the building's front door.

"Billy, I'm home now, and I have to go. But I'll be careful. Don't worry."

"Emma, wait. I'm not sure about—"

"I'll talk to you soon, and I'll see you in a few days. Bye."

I felt slightly guilty for hanging up on Billy when he was only trying to look out for me, but I had bigger issues to deal with. I needed to figure out which of my neighbors had helped Blanche create her website.

I stood in the lobby, trying to think about what my next move would be, when Mable Abernathy's door cracked open, and the wrinkled old woman popped her head out. Of course. Who knew more about the lives of the building's tenants than the woman who had lived her the longest?

"Oh, you already have breakfast. I was going to offer you a muffin," she said, sounding disappointed.

"Lucky for you, I'm still hungry," I said, winking.

Her parched lips pulled back in a smile, and she disappeared into the apartment, returning a second later with a giant poppy seed muffin in her hands.

I grabbed it, pulled back the paper, and took a big bite, barely containing a moan. "This is delicious, Mable."

She smiled. "I'm glad you like it. I love baking, but there's no way I could eat it all by myself. I love living in this apartment because I get to share with everyone who walks through the door. It's a great way to keep up with everyone."

"I'm sure it is," I said, thinking there would be no better transition into my question than that. "Actually, I wonder if you wouldn't be able to help me find someone."

"Of course, dear. Who are you looking for?" she asked, eyebrows raised.

"I'm not sure, actually. I know Blanche hired someone in the building to create the website, and I was wondering—"

"Oh, I hate that confounded thing," Mable said, interrupting me. "I can never manage to log in. I wrote down my name and passcode, but it never works properly. I always had to call Blanche down to help me log in, and she would get so crabby about it. If you ask me, the fellow she got to design it didn't do a very good job."

"That is frustrating," I said, frowning in sympathy. "Do you happen to know who she hired to design it?"

"Like I said, if you're looking to hire the same person for a project, I'd suggest you look elsewhere. I've lived here for over twenty years, and this is the most trouble I've ever had paying my rent. Blanche even tried to claim I was a few months behind, even though I always pay on the first of the month. The system is full of bugs."

"No, I need to find them to discuss something else. I'm not looking to create any websites anytime soon."

She nodded, eyes still narrowed. This was the most upset I'd ever seen Mable. Usually, she was always chipper and friendly. "It was the young man on the fifth floor, apartment 5C. Stephen, I believe was his name."

"Thank you so much, Mable. You've been very helpful."

"Of course, dear." She began closing the door behind her, and then stopped, looking back at me. "If the topic of the website does come up, you'll pass along my concerns, won't you? I'd love to go back to paying by checks."

"Of course, I will," I said, though I had absolutely no intention of telling a website designer that an elderly woman would rather pay by check than online.

"If you happen to come back by later, I may have a slice of pie for you. I'm working on a new pumpkin pie recipe."

I made a mental note of that. If it was good, I'd ask her for the recipe to pass on to my grandma. Grandma could be prideful, especially when it came to her baking, but there was nothing she loved more than beating Margene Huffler. I knew she'd take help from wherever she could get it.

12

After finishing off the rest of Mable's delicious lemon and poppy seed muffin, I showered, slipped into my favorite pair of jeans and a dark gray sweater, and then walked up the two flights of stairs to the fifth floor. The fluorescent light in the hallway was broken, casting the landing in stark shadows. I could see lights coming out from each of the units, and it smelled strongly of curry or some other spicy dish.

Unlike Mable, I had never made much of an effort to know my neighbors. I was content to move quietly in and out of the building, talking to no one, and going about my business. Now, however, when my investigation into Blanche's sudden death required a good deal of talking with my fellow tenants, I suddenly wished I'd been a bit more social.

5C was at the end of the hall, shrouded in so much darkness I almost missed the door and knocked on the brick wall next to it.

The door opened and a young man with vibrant blue

hair and a black hoodie on opened the door. He smiled broadly, defying my expectations. "How can I help you?"

"Oh, hi," I said, trying to fend off my surprise. "I'm Emma. I live on the third floor."

He held out his hand. "Stephen. Nice to meet you, Emma. Are you new to the building?"

I shook my head. "I've lived here for about three years, I think."

His smile faltered slightly. "Me too. I'm surprised I haven't seen you around."

"I'm not exactly a socializer," I said, being honest.

"Okay, then I should assume you are here for a serious purpose if it isn't a social call?" he asked, crossing his arms.

"Nothing too serious," I said, smiling so he wouldn't shut me out before I could even start the conversation. "I heard you were the person who created the website for the building?"

He groaned. "If you have an issue with the site, you need to take it up with Blanche's son, okay? I'm not an IT guy. I created the site, but I'm not here to troubleshoot it. Maybe if she'd paid me a fair price, I'd be more understanding, but I didn't make enough to be dealing with tenant issues two years later."

"No, the site is fine," I said. "Or, at least, last I checked it was fine. I've just heard that you know your way around a computer."

He raised a light eyebrow, tilting his head to the side. "I guess that's true."

"Okay. Well, it might seem strange, but I'm trying to find a cabbie. A specific cabbie, but I have no idea where to start. I thought maybe there would be a database somewhere online...a way to contact them."

"You want to find a cabbie?" he asked, both eyebrows

lifted nearly to his hairline now, his head tipped forward until his chin was resting on his chest.

"Correct."

"Did you used to date one?" he asked. "Or does one of them owe you money?"

I laughed. "No, nothing like that."

He twisted his mouth to the side, looking me up and down as though assessing the likelihood that I was hiding weapons on my person. "Do you have money?"

I nodded. "Cash."

His face spread into a slow smile, and then he stood back, throwing his door open and letting me come inside. "Welcome to Casa Becket."

Stephen Becket's apartment would have been very tidy if it hadn't been for the mess of chords that stretched from his large corner computer desk to the cable port in the wall above the kitchen counter.

"Mind the cords," he said, gesturing at the river of cables as if I could have missed them. "The worst thing about these old apartments is that there aren't enough outlets and they aren't designed for modern day technology. I have to use my ethernet cable to get a decent signal in this brick prison."

"Oh, yeah," I said, trying to sympathize. I'd always done most of my out-of-office design work at coffee shops or the library, so the internet speed in the building had never been a serious concern of mine. Once I was off work for the day, I was so tired of looking at a computer that I'd usually spend the evening in bed watching a movie or reading a book. "The worst."

Stephen hopped over the thick rope of electricity and plopped down in a well-padded computer chair. His computer was already on and humming. It was obvious he spent a lot of time in front of it.

"Okay, you are actually in a lot of luck here because I once had a bit of a feud with a taxi driver."

"Okay?" I said, a question in my voice. "How does that help me?"

He looked over his shoulder and smiled at me. "Because I play dirty, my friend. The driver ripped me off and thought he could get away with it. So, I contacted the New York City Taxi and Limousine Commission. That's the agency within the city government that regulates the for-hire vehicle industry. If you want the name of a driver, that's the place to go. Of course, government bureaucracy means they won't willingly release private information to citizens, so I had to enter through the backdoor, if you know what I mean." He winked at me.

"You hacked in?"

He nodded. "You betcha. It was easier than you'd expect. I had the cab number and a name. Raul Gonzales found himself on the no-flyers list next time he went to the airport. Suspected terrorist activity."

"You got him in trouble with the federal government?" I asked, suddenly wondering whether I wasn't in over my head. What would Stephen do to me when he realized I only had fifty dollars in cash in my pocket? Would I be able to fly back to Missouri?

"It wasn't the first time," he said with a shrug. "So, anyway, you're lucky because I like to leave my little backdoors unlocked for future use. It will only take me a minute to kick it open and get you what you need. Do you have a cab number?"

"No, just a name," I said.

"Okay, let's have it."

"Ernest."

His fingers stopped typing, the room falling into a heavy silence. "Ernest what?"

"I only have a first name."

Suddenly, Stephen spun around in his chair and crossed his hands over his stomach. "You only have a first name?"

"Is that bad?"

He looked at me like I was a child and sighed before turning back around. "It isn't good. For your sake, you better hope Ernest is an unpopular name. I can narrow down the list, but I won't be able to give you any specifics."

"Anything will help," I said.

Stephen's fingers flew across the keyboard faster than I thought possible. Screens opened and closed before I could even tell what was on them.

"So," Stephen said, his fingers still moving a mile a minute. "Did Blanche tell you I designed the website? Before she died, I mean?"

I found it weird that he added that caveat. Did he expect Blanche to have been able to tell me anything *after* she died? Surely, he didn't have any clue about the ghostly visions I'd been seeing, so it seemed strange for him to make it clear that it'd have to have been before her death. I brushed it off, though.

"No, I asked around a bit," I said.

"Mable?"

I laughed. "Yeah. How did you know?"

"That old lady knows everything. And she doesn't have to hack into anything to figure it out. She's observant."

"That she is," I said.

"But I would have been surprised if Blanche had given you my name. She wasn't my biggest fan," he said.

"She asked you to design the website, though?"

"Yeah, but things went South from there." He smiled. "Let's just say, Blanche believed I was abusing my power."

I wrinkled my forehead, wondering how someone could abuse their power over an apartment building website, when suddenly, I remembered something.

"The graphics," I said, my voice trailing off.

Stephen looked over his shoulder again, grinning at me.

"The panda pooping on the home page? The frog that flipped you off on the log in page?"

He nodded to both. "I thought they were funny, but Blanche got really upset. Really, *really* upset. She kept asking me to stop messing with the site and kept changing the password, but I had already set up my back door. She couldn't keep me out. So, she blackmailed me."

"What do you mean?"

"I mean, she found some dirt on me and threatened to tell the police if I ever did it again. Blackmail."

"Oh," I said, desperately wishing I could ask Stephen what dirt she had to hold over him. But I knew he wouldn't tell me. Why would he? If he didn't want Blanche to have the information, he surely wouldn't tell me anything about it.

"Somehow Blanche found out about one of my previous hacks. You remember when I said I put Raul Gonzales on the no-fly list?"

I nodded.

"Well, that was easy because I already had the back door."

My jaw fell open. "You hacked the government? You had a back door to the National Security Agency?"

He shrugged like it was no big deal, but I could see the smirk on his face. "It was just a prank to see if I could pull it off. But Blanche found out about it and threatened to tell the government. I would do a few years in federal, at least. And they'd have eyes on my online activity forever. It would have totally ruined my career. So, I stopped the stupid graphics. She also increased my rent by one hundred dollars a month, which totally sucked."

"How did Blanche find out information like that?" I asked. Blanche was a divorced, former housewife, who spent most of her time in her apartment, watching reruns of old TV shows. Her television had rabbit ears and a staticky screen. She wasn't exactly tech-savvy.

"I have no idea. I definitely didn't tell her. Maybe she has a connection with someone who can dig up dirt on people. I don't know."

Up until that point, I'd felt as though Stephen had been honest with me. But now I had a strong feeling he was lying. The only things I had to go off of were his suddenly nervous behavior and the fact that he had just revealed the secret that could get him locked away in federal prison to me, a relative stranger. So, if he had been willing to brag about his illegal escapades to me, he had probably done the same with Blanche, and she had decided to use the information to get what she wanted.

Part of me was proud of Blanche for standing up for herself, but another part of me was busy formulating a theory. What if Blanche had been using her information on Stephen for more than just stopping vulgar cartoons from appearing on her business' website? What if she had been blackmailing him into working for her? I had no idea what Blanche would have wanted Stephen to do, but if she'd been willing to blackmail him once, it seemed likely she wouldn't have had an issue doing it again. Could he have grown sick of being a puppet and ended her once and for all? Or, had Blanche finally decided to share the information she had on him, causing him to silence her forever?

The theory seemed dark, especially since Stephen seemed like a genuinely nice guy, blue spiky hair and all. But if Blanche's autopsy came back as anything other than a natural death, every possibility had to be explored. And anyone Blanche was blackmailing would immediately be pretty high on the list of suspects.

"Okay," Stephen said, startling me from my suspicious thoughts. "I have a list of every cabbie in New York City who goes by Ernest, Ernesto, or Ernie. Sixty-seven names."

He rolled his chair away from his desk and moved towards the printer that took up half of his kitchen counter. Three pages of paper rolled out. He picked them up, tapped them once against the counter to align them, and then held them out towards me.

I grabbed them and shoved them down into my purse. "How much do you charge?"

He tossed his head back and forth, looking up towards the ceiling in thought. "Because I already had the back door set up and you were fun to talk to, we'll call it a cool forty. First time buyer's discount," he said with a wink.

I resisted the urge to sigh with relief and pulled the forty dollars out of my purse. "Thanks for all your help."

Stephen walked me towards his apartment door, but before I could reach for the handle, he slid in front of it, blocking my path.

I pulled my hand back, my entire body suddenly pulsing with adrenaline. What was he doing? I'd paid him, he'd handed over the information. What was going on?

"You never said what you plan to do with Ernest," he said, eyes narrowed.

"Just looking for an old friend," I lied.

I could tell he didn't believe me, but I didn't care. All I cared about was making it out of his apartment and back into the hallway. The dark hallway. The dark, deserted hallway. Really, all I cared about was making it back to my apartment and locking the door behind me.

Stephen took a step towards me, a hand running nervously through his blue hair. "You can tell me. I told you a secret. You owe me."

"I didn't ask for your secret," I said. "You offered it up."

"Well how do I know you won't tell anyone if you don't tell me a secret of your own?" he asked, mouth curled up in a sinister smile.

I shoved one of my hands into my purse and clutched the taser in my bag. "I won't tell anyone. And you can believe me because I'm not a liar. And since you now know I'm not a liar, I'd like to make it abundantly clear to you that I have a charged taser in my purse that could bring an elephant to its knees. So, I highly suggest you step out of my way and let me pass."

Stephen's smile faded, and his eyes widened. "Whoa. That got serious fast. I was just kidding."

"I wasn't," I said. "Please move."

He stepped away from the door, and without looking back, I threw it open and darted down the dark hallway and down the stairs. I didn't stop moving until I made it to my apartment and locked the door. As soon as I did, my phone began to ring. Body still thrumming with adrenaline, I saw that it was an unknown number and felt certain it was Stephen. Somehow, he'd hacked into my phone and knew my number. He was going to kill me the way he had Blanche. As much as I wanted to ignore it, I couldn't. I had to know.

"Hello?" I asked, voice shaky.

"What's crack-a-lackin, pretty lady?" Tucker's goofy drawl was the exact opposite of what I'd expected, and I nearly burst out laughing. "I was thinking we'd hit the town today. Are you ready?"

I closed my eyes and sighed, letting my heart rate return to normal.

"Sure, Tucker. Let's hit the town."

13

Twenty minutes later, I was in Williamsburg with a very overwhelmed Larry Tucker.

To his credit, Tucker looked the part. Tall and blonde with a chiseled jawline. He looked like every other young, handsome man walking down the street. He drew the eye of all of the women passing by in black and denim. In fact, he looked more like a New Yorker than I did. Even after a few years in the city, I was still mistaken for a tourist occasionally.

However, Tucker was obviously out of his depth. His brows were constantly furrowed, his forehead wrinkled in confusion. We passed by artisan soap and cheese shops, storefronts that displayed leather beanies and wool finger-less gloves in the windows. We walked into one clothing store and Tucker took one look at the exposed burnished pipes and naked lightbulbs hanging by wires from the ceiling and assumed the store was closed for repairs.

"No, it's open," I said.

"But..." he pointed to the raw two-by-fours screwed into the walls and the unfinished concrete floor.

"It's designed that way," I assured him, gesturing to the other customers who were milling around the shop.

We eventually walked through the store, but it was obvious Tucker still wasn't convinced by my evidence. He seemed afraid to touch anything in case it wasn't actually for sale, and he would be accused of stealing. I wanted to tease him, but it made sense. Hillbilly Hollow's most hip store was definitely Suzy's boutique, but even that had a small-town vibe. The clothes, while fashionable, hung on metal hangers on metal racks, and the dressing room was just a series of thick curtains hanging from the ceiling. Tucker didn't have much experience with boutique stores, especially not the hipster ones in Williamsburg.

He did end up buying a few things. He bought his dad an "I Love NYC" snow globe, and he bought all of the Hillbilly Hollow officers a pendant of the Statue of Liberty to hang from the rearview mirrors of their cars. I tried a few times to have him buy something for himself from one of the shops, but after he walked into a store with ripped leather pants and a fringe denim vest, he decided he didn't need anything fancier than what the big box store back home could offer.

"I'm happy to just take it all in," he insisted. "You shop wherever you like, and I'll have a good time."

It felt strange walking down the street with Tucker right next to me. Shopping felt distinctly like a couple activity. I had the sense that everyone we passed assumed we were together, and the fact that I was shopping for a bridesmaid dress didn't help matters. The sales associate at one shop brought me a different size in a dress and a matching bow tie for my "boyfriend." I corrected her quickly and sent her away before Tucker could notice. The last thing he needed was any encouragement.

Even though he wasn't making any more obvious attempts to woo me, I knew he still had hopes that something romantic would arise between us. And as nice as he was, I knew it would never happen. I just hadn't found the right way to break the news to him yet. Plus, if I told him too early, it would make the rest of the trip an awkward nightmare. I just needed to keep things casual until we were back in Missouri and I could let him down gently.

"Emma," Tucker said from behind me, sounding breathless. "That one looks beautiful on you."

Tucker had been waiting outside the dressing room for me to come out in a dress for ten minutes, but I kept telling him they didn't look right to avoid having to show him, so he'd eventually left. As soon as I was sure he'd wandered off to find something to occupy himself with, I poked my head out of the dressing room and used the three-paned full body mirror in the lounge area rather than the single six-foot tall mirror hanging on the back of the dressing room door. Apparently, however, Tucker hadn't wandered off as far as I'd hoped.

"Really, you look like a princess. Better than the bride, I bet."

I gave him a friendly smile. "I don't think that would be welcome news to the bride. I think she'll want to be the best dressed woman at her own wedding."

"Okay, well maybe not as good as the bride, then," he said, his mouth turned up in a crooked grin. "But I reckon it'd be pretty close."

After trying on close to twenty navy dresses, they were all beginning to look the same, but I thought I agreed with Tucker about this one. The neckline was wide and cut across the tops of my shoulders, giving the dress a vintage kind of look, but the lace overlay made it look timeless. The fabric clung close to my chest and ribs, and then flared out at my waist, cutting off at the middle of my shin.

"Thanks, Tucker."

"Are you gonna get that one?" he asked.

I hummed, uncertain. "I don't know yet."

For as nice as Tucker was being, I noticed his shoulders visibly droop. He had endured just about as much dress shopping as he could handle.

"You can go explore a bit if you want," I offered. "I might try a few of these on again before I make my final decision."

Tucker looked towards the door longingly and then back at me. "I don't want to leave you."

"We have our cell phones. I'll call you when I'm done." I shooed him away with a brush of my hands and he took a step towards the door.

"Are you sure?" he asked.

I nodded. "I noticed a street performer at the end of the block. You could go listen to a few songs."

"Okay. If you insist. Just call me when you're ready and I'll come right back."

The poor man practically sprinted from the store.

Really, there was a ninety-nine percent chance I was going to buy the navy dress I was wearing. It was by far the most beautiful one I'd seen all day. I just needed a few Tucker-free moments to take care of something. I snapped a picture of myself in the mirror and then sent it to Suzy and Billy in separate messages.

I was in the middle of drafting a message to Billy when Suzy's text came back seconds later.

SUZY: YES! YES YES YES! That is the one. If U don't buy it, I'm kicking U out of Annie's wedding.

ME: I'm buying it! Don't let her replace me with another bridesmaid!

I CLICKED BACK to Billy's conversation. Three dots at the bottom of the screen showed me he was typing, and then they went away. They reappeared again, and then flicked away. Clearly, Billy was speechless. I smiled as I finished my text to him.

ME: I found a dress for the wedding! Were U serious about me buying U a suit because I don't think it will fit in my carry on? (: I have a favor 2 ask. Call me when U get the chance.

I HAD JUST SLIPPED out of the dress and back into my jeans and sweater when my phone rang. It was Billy.

"Hello, Doctor Will."

He laughed. "Hi Emma. First of all, I can find my own suit, but thanks for double-checking. And second," there was a long pause where I wondered whether the thick brick walls of the store had interfered with reception. "You look beautiful in that dress."

My cheeks warmed, making me glad we were on the phone and not talking in person. "Thank you. I had to try on a million dresses, but I finally found a winner. Suzy likes it, too."

"Did Tucker help you pick it out?" he asked, his tone only half-teasing. Before I could respond, he sighed. "Sorry.

You've explained the situation multiple times, and I need to let it go. Tell Tucker hi from me."

"I would, but he isn't here right now," I said softly. "He was getting tired of dress shopping."

"Amateur," Billy said, sounding much more chipper.

"Completely," I agreed.

"So, what do you need from me?" he asked.

"I know you're at work right now, so I don't expect you to drop everything and help me out, but I need help with a bit of research."

"Is the internet not as good over there in the big city as it is back in Hillbilly Hollow or something?" he teased.

"Well, Hillbilly Hollow is free of Larry Tucker, which makes it the perfect place to conduct this secret research."

Billy lowered his voice, even though Tucker wasn't around, and even if he was, he wouldn't have been able to hear Billy. "You don't want Tucker to know about what you're looking up?"

I nodded. "Yes, exactly."

"Okay, I can do that. What do you need me to do?"

"I have a list of taxi drivers in New York City that could be the man who ran me over a few months back, but I need you to help me weed some of them out."

Billy sighed. "I don't know, Emma..."

I knew Billy didn't approve of my search for the cab driver who had hit me, but I also knew he would find a small level of satisfaction from the fact that he was helping me with a project that was being kept secret from Tucker. I was hoping that would be enough to convince him to help. Because I really didn't want Tucker to find out just yet. If he did, he would surely try to stop me. Or, because he was a sheriff himself, he might force me to go to the police. And while I did want closure where the accident was concerned,

I didn't necessarily want to press charges. It would be easier to handle this the way I wanted if I kept Tucker out of it for as long as possible.

"I'll do it with or without you, Billy," I said. "But I'd rather do it with you."

I could hear him breathing on the other end of the phone, and then he let out a sigh of resignation. "Okay, I'm on board."

I resisted the urge to celebrate, and instead took a deep breath. "Thanks, Billy. I can always count on you. I'll send you a list of the names and addresses. The guy I had help me found everyone by the name of Ernest, Ernesto, and Ernie. But the cab driver who hit me went by 'Ernest,' so I think you can just stick to those. Doing that will leave twelve names. I'm looking for a guy with curly dark hair and a thick black beard that touches his chest."

"The guy that helped you?" Billy asked. "Who got you this list?"

"Just a hacker in my apartment building."

"A hacker?" he said, sounding disbelieving. "Are you sure you aren't taking this too far, Emma? I don't want you involved with any dangerous people."

So, that was a clear sign that I definitely shouldn't tell Billy that Stephen had been extremely threatening as I'd left his apartment. I didn't need him to know exactly how much danger I was putting myself into.

"He's just your run of the mill tech geek. He helped me get a list of names from a city database. Easy peasy."

"Maybe if that city was Hillbilly Hollow. But this was in New York. I'm sure there was a lot more standing between him and that information than a password of 1234."

"Are you still on board or not?" I asked, peeking through

the curtain to be sure Tucker hadn't snuck back into the dressing room while I was distracted.

"Yes, I'll help. I just wish I was there with you," he said. I could imagine him running his hand anxiously through his hair the way he always did. "Promise me you'll take Tucker with you."

"Now you want me spending time with Tucker?" I teased.

"Em, promise. Please."

I could hear the concern in his voice, the worry. Billy really did care about my safety. In that moment, I wished he was there with me, too. If it was him instead of Tucker, I wouldn't have hesitated to have him help me track down Ernest or solve Blanche's murder. He worried about me, but Billy never held me back.

Just as I was about to open my mouth, I lifted my head to look in the mirror and was met with a pale white apparition instead. Startled, I jolted backwards, slamming into the partition between my dressing room and the next. Blanche was standing in front of me, her hair frizzy around her face, eyes wide and focused on me.

I wondered why she didn't speak. True, Preacher Jacob's ghost had never been talkative, but the spirits of Melody Campbell and Prudence Huffler had always had plenty to say. Still, every ghost was different, I supposed.

I could see my breath. The dressing room had become unbearably cold all of a sudden. My teeth chattered.

"Emma? Are you there?"

I could hear Billy talking in my ear, but the conversation felt like another lifetime. Staring at Blanche's foggy form in front of me, nothing in the real world seemed to matter.

I blinked a few times, trying to focus. When the spirits

appeared, it was usually to deliver a message, to give me a clue. I needed to pay attention.

"Emma?" Billy was becoming more and more frustrated on the end of the line, his voice wavering somewhere between panic and anger.

Squeezing my eyes shut, I spun away from Blanche, facing the opposite wall, and tried to forget she was there, though the hair on the back of my neck was standing up. For some reason, this ghost creeped me out in a way the others never had.

"I promise," I said in a rush, not entirely sure whether I meant it or not. "I'll take Tucker with me."

"Okay, good. Send me the information. I had a couple cancellations this afternoon, so I'll get back to you pretty quickly, assuming I'm able to find stuff on all of these guys."

"You're a lifesaver, Billy. Thank you. I'll send everything right now."

"You owe me," Billy said.

That was the second time I'd heard that phrase that day, but luckily it sounded much better coming from Billy than it had from Stephen.

"I know."

When I hung up, I held the phone to my chest for a second, half-hoping that when I turned around, Blanche would be gone. I took a deep breath.

As I expected because of the icy chill racing up my spine, Blanche was still standing behind me. Just as she had been on the street the night before with Tucker, she was moving her mouth but no sound was coming out.

"I don't understand what you're trying to tell me," I whispered. "If this is a clue, I'm not getting it. I need something else."

Blanche's eyes stayed blankly fixed on me, looking through me rather than at me.

"Was your death foul play?" I asked. "It would help if you could say something aloud."

Maybe she didn't like being criticized for her silence. Blanche's eyes shot open wide, her mouth flattened into a hard line, and then just as she had every other time I'd seen her, she flickered once and then disappeared.

14

If the sales associate overheard me talking to myself in the dressing room, she didn't mention it while she rang up the navy-blue dress for me and placed it in a black garment bag. I draped the bag over my arm and walked out into the day. It was warm, especially in contrast to the ghostly chill of the dressing room, and I stopped in the doorway to let the sun spread over me like a blanket.

I took a deep breath and was surprised by the staleness of the air, the smell of car exhaust and of the nearby garbage can. I'd lived in New York for years, but a few months back on the farm had made me used to the smell of nature. I missed it. Much more than I thought I would. Even though I'd been hesitant to head back to New York City so soon after moving to Missouri, part of me had still expected to enjoy the trip more. But as every day passed, I was more tempted to forget about Blanche's possible murder and go back to the farm. However, if Blanche's boldness was any sign, she wouldn't let me forget about her. I had to solve this puzzle if I wanted any amount of peace.

"There you are."

I turned to see Tucker leaning against the brick wall of the boutique. His arms were crossed over his chest, and he looked like a real New Yorker in every way.

"I'm hungry. Are you ready for lunch?" he asked.

"Almost," I said.

He raised an eyebrow. "Almost?"

"Would you be too put out if I stopped to buy a matching pair of shoes before we leave?" I asked, wincing.

I could see the disappointment cross his face, but always the gentleman, Tucker smiled. "Course not. You can't very well be a bridesmaid without a pair of shoes."

I ducked into a shop two doors down that looked like it would be my best shot at finding the strappy pair of nude heels I had in mind. I browsed the displays as quickly as possible, trying not to let myself get distracted by the seemingly endless pairs of beautiful shoes. So beautiful I wanted to stop and admire each pair for the piece of artwork it was. But I resisted. That was, until Shonda, the sales associate caught me.

"You look like a woman who knows her way around a shoe," she said, pouting her purple lips at me.

"I have a good-sized collection," I admitted. Though, I had almost no occasion to wear most of them now that I was back on the farm. There weren't very many places in Hillbilly Hollow where my black and red stilettos would be appropriate. I'd seriously contemplated wearing them to church with an overly-conservative black wrap dress, but it was a lost cause. The women in grandma's quilting circle would have been whispering behind my back for a month.

"Then you have got to see the new pair of boots we got in just last night. They're going to be the perfect wedge boot to get you from Fall to Winter. You can dress them up or down. Honestly, my favorite thing in the shop right now."

Nothing got my heart racing like a good wedge boot, but I could practically feel Tucker glaring at Shonda over my shoulder, willing her to go back behind the counter and leave us alone.

"I'm actually looking for a nude heel," I said. "It's for a bridesmaid dress. So, nothing too flashy."

She clapped her hands together. "I have the exact right thing in the back. I can also grab you that boot if you'd like?"

I wavered between a yes and a no for a few seconds, a war between my head and my heart, and like any good predator, Shonda saw my weakness.

"I'll grab it just in case." She looked down at my shoes. "What are you, a seven-and-a-half?"

I nodded. "Good eye."

She winked at me and then whisked to the back of the store.

"The sales people here are aggressive," Tucker said. "I buy my shoes at the same place I buy my groceries, though, so I reckon I don't have a lot of experience in this area."

A laugh burst out of me before I could stop it. "I'm sorry, I don't mean to laugh. It's just funny how different things are here than back home."

Tucker nodded slowly like he was thinking. "I see why people like New York. It's big. Lots of fancy shops and places and people. Always somethin' to do. But now that I'm here, I don't know if I understand why *you* like it."

I sat down on a try-on bench and slipped out of my sneakers. "What do you mean?"

"Well, you don't seem to know very many of your neighbors, and we've stayed pretty close to your apartment for food and stuff. It doesn't seem like you like going out very much." He held up both hands, palms out. "I could be wrong, that's just what I've seen so far."

Part of me wanted to be offended, but Tucker was right. My old job at the ad agency had been mostly solitary work, and I hadn't been close with many co-workers. Even though I was desperate for more friends the entire time I lived in the city, I only became close with a few girls from a spin class I went to twice a week and Shelby, who used to be a barista at my favorite coffee shop. I got together with each of them once or twice a month, but otherwise I spent my time alone. Even my one-time roommate hadn't lasted long. New York City—Brooklyn, especially—was supposed to be this mecca for young professionals to meet and mingle, but I'd spend most of my time reading books and watching television.

"No apology necessary," I said. "You're right. I guess I never did make the most of my time here."

"Ya seem at home in Missouri, though," he said. "It suits you. Plus, I like runnin' into you around town. It feels like the good old days."

I didn't quite understand which good old days Tucker was referring to considering he and I had never hung out in high school, but I ignored this.

"I like being back, too. But you know, I've thought quite a few times that you seem very at home here."

"In New York?" he asked, both eyebrows raised. "Really?"

I nodded. "Is that hard to believe?"

"Well, maybe not hard to believe. Just surprisin'. If I see one more man bun or hookah lounge, I think I'll go crazy." He laughed. "It's a fun place to visit, but I wouldn't wanna live here."

Shonda returned with four boxes of shoes balanced in her arms, an apologetic smile on her face. "I may have gotten carried away back there, but I really think you're going to love what I pulled for you."

Tucker let out a small groan and settled his back against the wall. Clearly, he had realized there was no sense in fighting a losing battle.

I tried on the nude heels first and immediately knew they were exactly what I wanted. The straps were thick and covered most of my foot, making them conservative, but they still had a very Spring vibe that would work well with the dress.

Then, I slipped on the wedge boots. Until that moment, I had never been the kind of person to believe in destiny, but as soon as that shoe settled upon my foot, I knew it was meant to be. They were black with a bright silver zipper running diagonally up the side. I could see them pairing well with my jeans or a wrap dress and jean jacket—the perfect shoe for casual or formal, Winter or Spring.

"Did I tell you or did I tell you?" Shonda asked, eyes wide and knowing.

"Are those even going to fit in your luggage?" Tucker asked.

"I'll throw everything else away," I said, turning my leg one way and then the other, admiring my new favorite inanimate object.

"Should I go ahead and wrap both of these up?" Shonda asked, holding up the boxes for the heels and the wedges.

I was just about to tell her to wait so I could try on the other pair of knee-high brown boots she'd brought me when I felt my phone vibrate once, twice, a third time, and a fourth. All at once, I remembered what I'd asked Billy to do and realized what the texts likely were. Disregarding everyone around me, I yanked my phone out of my pocket and quickly read the messages.

BILLY: A few of the Ernests on the list are no longer working as cabbies and another didn't start driving a cab until after your accident if his social media is 2 be believed. So, that leaves 3 guys who roughly fit the description U gave. I'm sending their pictures now.

[OPEN IMAGE]

[OPEN IMAGE]

[OPEN IMAGE]

I VAGUELY HEARD someone talking in the background, but I was too busy opening the pictures Billy had sent to pay attention. The first was a pale white man hidden behind a lot of dark brown hair. He looked like a man wearing a costume of a caveman. His hair was parted down the center and the beard stuck out in a mess of untamed fly-aways. Definitely not the Ernest I'd seen the day of my accident.

The second photo popped up, and this one made me pause. My immediate reaction was that the man was not the same one driving the cab that hit me or the man at the airport. However, how good of a look had I really gotten in both situations? Just glimpses. Couldn't this man just as easily be the right Ernest as the wrong one? I wanted to just skip to the third photo, but I didn't want to pollute my already muddled mind. If I added another face, I would only become less certain. I needed to make a definitive yes or no determination before moving onto the next photo.

It was like when I had the dream in high school that Billy took me to the high school dance. The dream started out normally enough, but the longer it went on, the more Billy started to look like my grandpa. And the bizarre thing was that my dream self didn't seem to mind. I just continued to slow dance with the horror movie mash up of the boy next door and my grandpa. I didn't want this same confusing mix-up to happen with the photos Billy had found and the picture I had in my head. I needed to try and keep them as separate as possible.

The man had a deep tan and lines around his eyes and mouth that signified a lot of sun damage or a lot of laughter, I couldn't be sure which. His hair was the right color—black like a suit button—but the texture seemed wrong. It looked more woolly than I remembered, but what if the photo was taken during a particularly humid season or when he'd run out of his favorite styling product?

I squinted at the image, trying to imagine seeing the face through the dirty windshield of a New York City cab, and I made my decision. It wasn't him. The decision was based more on instinct than any hard facts, but I felt confident. I'd know the man if I saw him again.

"Emma? What's wrong?" Tucker was standing in front of me now, bending down to look me in the eyes.

"What?" I asked, clicking my screen to black so he wouldn't see the photo still there.

Tucker narrowed his eyes. "Shonda asked if you wanted her to wrap up your shoes."

"Just the nude heels," I said. "Thanks."

Shonda pouted. "I thought the wedges were a win."

"Just the heels," I repeated more firmly this time. "Thanks."

Shonda left and I thought I saw her roll her eyes as she walked away, but I couldn't be bothered to care. I still had one more picture to look at.

"Are you okay?" Tucker asked.

I smiled. "Just low blood sugar, I think. Too many shoes, not enough protein. Do you want to go get us a car while I pay?"

Tucker had shown clear discomfort at having to hail cabs since being in New York, but I must have looked shaken enough that he decided not to argue. He just nodded and disappeared through the front doors of the shop.

Now alone again, I pulled out my phone. The wrong Ernest's face filled my screen for a second before I flicked it away. I clicked on the third photo, and just as I'd suspected, I recognized him instantly. He was the one. The man who hit me and drove away, leaving me in the street. The man who recognized me at the airport and fled in fear. He was the right Ernest, and there was no mistaking it. Billy had found him.

ME: Third one. Definitely.

DURING THE FEW minutes it took for me to pay for the shoes and make awkward chit chat with a much less friendly Shonda, Billy messaged me back with Ernest Adrian's information. He was thirty-two, had been driving a cab for five years, and had several prior vehicular incidents, involving speeding and reckless driving. Billy also sent his cab number and the number to his cab company.

BILLY: Like I said, U owe me.
    BILLY: Be careful.
    BILLY: Please.
    ME: Thanks. I will.

I LOOKED through the glass window of the shop and saw

Tucker standing awkwardly by the curb. A whole host of other people were hopping in and out of cabs, but he stood back politely, letting them move ahead of him. I only had a minute or two, but it had to be enough time.

I ducked behind one of the shoe displays, punched in the number for the cab company that Billy had sent me, and let it ring a few times.

"Big Apple Cab. This is Julia."

"Hi Julia," I said, my voice so sickly sweet I could have given myself a cavity. "My name is...Margene Huffler." I didn't know what made me grab Margene's name out of nowhere, but for some reason I felt uncomfortable giving up my real identity.

"Hello *Margene*," Julia said, judgment clear in her voice. I didn't love the name, either, but I was still surprised by her open disapproval. "How can I help you?"

"I was the world's biggest idiot and lost an earring in the back of one of your cabs."

"Give me the name of your driver and your address. I'll pass along the information and if the driver finds your item, it will be mailed back to you within the week." It was clear Julia spent a large portion of her day repeating this same sentence over and over again, and she wasn't going to take kindly to me pushing back against the process.

"I'm sorry to be trouble," I said. "But I don't have a week. In fact, I don't even have a day. I need that earring tonight. I'm desperate."

"I'm sorry, but you're going to have to find another pair that match your outfit, because this is our protocol for lost items," she said.

I inhaled and began to launch into a long-winded and not at all planned rant. "The earring is a family heirloom—my great grandmother's on my mom's side—and it was loaned to me by my mom a few months ago. We have a rehearsal dinner for my sister's wedding tonight, and I told my mom I would be wearing the earrings. Now, I could just tell her I changed my mind and decided to wear a different pair, but then I'll spend the entire evening hearing about how much better the heirloom earrings would have looked than the ones I chose. And all of this will lead to the inevitable line: 'Your sister really wanted those earrings, but because you're the eldest, I gave them to you. If you aren't going to wear them, then you should do the right thing and give them to Marcy.'"

"Margene and Marcy?" Julia asked.

"We're twins," I said. "I'm older by ten minutes."

Julia groaned in a surprising show of sympathy before letting me continue.

"So, if I don't get this earring back immediately, my sister's wedding will shift from being a terrible night where everyone in my family tries to hide that she's really their favorite to a downright horrible night where everyone in my family openly admits that I'm their least favorite, and the earrings will be listed as the main reason. So, please, can you help me out?"

There was a long pause where I wondered if Julia had heard enough of my rant and decided to hang up, but then she chuckled. "Families, am I right? Nothing makes you crazier."

"You got that right," I said.

"Okay, I don't usually do this," she said. "But all our drivers have GPS in their cars, so if you give me the name of your driver then I can tell you the general location he's working right now. How is that?"

"Better than nothing," I said. I gave her the information and waited. A few minutes later, Julia came back on the line.

"Ernest is on lunch right now. He usually parks for the full hour, so if you can get to West 72nd and West End in the next forty minutes then you should be able to find him."

"Julia, you're a life saver," I said as I committed the address to memory.

"Make out with one of the groomsmen if you can," she said with a snicker. "That'll give them something to talk about."

If I'd had a few more minutes to spare, maybe I would have tried to chat with Julia a bit more. But, as it was, I had just enough time to get across town if I wanted to catch Ernest. I thanked her again, shoved the phone in my pocket, and stepped out onto the street with a renewed sense of purpose.

Tucker had already mentioned how closely we'd stuck to the area around my apartment, so even though I knew he was starving, it didn't take much prodding to convince him we should head to the West Village. I hailed a cab and directed the driver to a sushi restaurant I knew was close to where Julia had said Ernest would be.

"Sushi?" Tucker asked, looking nervous.

I nodded. "Have you ever had it before?"

He shook his head, eyes wide.

"Well, then you have to try it," I said. "Plus, if you're ever going to give it a try, it would be better to eat it here than back home. No offense to Hillbilly Hollow, but they don't know much about fish unless it's fried catfish."

"Do they have fried sushi?" Tucker asked.

"Actually, they do. Deep fried sushi rolls."

He hummed, unconvinced. "Maybe I'll try one of those."

After that, Tucker picked up the conversation, commenting on people and businesses and buildings as we passed, making observations and chuckling to himself. If he noticed that I wasn't paying much attention to the conversation, he didn't seem to mind, which was nice. I couldn't focus on anything other than the thrum of my own heart, the flip of my stomach. I'd been just as hungry as Tucker half an hour before, but now I felt hollow in a sick way—the way I always felt before I came down with the flu or a stomach bug. I felt like I could heave any second.

Was I ready to see Ernest again? I wanted closure, but was this the way to get it?

I knew my accident could have been so much worse. I could have been paralyzed or suffered brain damage—though, seeing ghosts did feel like a form of brain damage, if you asked me. But as it was, I still suffered nightmares about the accident. Barring the one incident with Tucker when I'd seen Blanche's ghost across the street, I was always nervous to step into traffic or cross the road when a car was within a block of me. Getting hit by Ernest's taxi had changed my life forever, and it didn't feel right that he could just walk away.

Twenty-three minutes later, our driver pulled up in front of NY Sushi. If Julia was to be believed, I had thirteen minutes before Ernest would flip his cab light back on and pull away from the curb. The sushi restaurant was in the middle of West 72nd, one block back from West End Avenue. One block away from Ernest.

The restaurant was at two-thirds capacity, and we were seated immediately at a table in the direct center of the room. The place looked like something out of a science fiction movie. Pink neon rope lights ran around the edge of the floor and the ceiling, black walls and floors added to the contrast and unrealistic feeling, and mirrors set into the wall behind the bar reflected the space back, making it seem endless.

"This is definitely somethin'," Tucker said, looking around. His usually tan skin looked pale in the wash of neon lights. In fact, he had taken on a blue pallor, much like many of the spirits I'd seen since my accident.

"There's a restaurant for everything in New York," I said. "Every cuisine, every mood, every atmosphere."

A waitress with chop sticks holding up a high bun on the back of her head brought us menus and water glasses. "Take a look at your menus, and I will be back in a few minutes to take your order."

Tucker was perusing his menu, eyes squinted at the text as though it was blurry and he was trying to bring it into focus. I needed to get away from him. We'd only been in the restaurant for four minutes—a surprisingly short time to be seated and handed a menu—and time was running out.

"I don't know what any of this means," Tucker said. "Why don't you just order for the both of us?"

"I can do that," I said absently.

Tucker smiled and dropped his menu. "Okay, great. That's a load off my shoulders."

"But I have to go," I added, standing up. "Just for a minute. I just remembered there's something I have to do."

"What?" Tucker asked, brow wrinkled. "You have to go somewhere?"

I nodded. "It's close. I'll be right back."

"I can go with ya," he said, scooting away from the table. "If it's so important, we can take care of it and then come back and eat."

I shook my head. "No, you stay. Hold our table. I'll be right back."

I could see the waitress moving across the restaurant

towards us, and I didn't want to get caught talking to her. I had seven minutes.

"But you were gonna order for us," Tucker said. "Emma, wait."

But I was already gone. As I slipped through the front door, I glanced back to see Tucker and the waitress both staring at me. I felt guilty for it, but I had to ignore them and jog off down the sidewalk.

Like most of New York, it was hard to turn your head without seeing several bright yellow taxis. They were a city staple. But in that moment, I hated them all. I needed one specific taxi. One specific driver. Julia had said Ernest would be at the corner of West 72nd and West End, so I jogged the length of the block and stood at the corner, swiveling and arching my neck to look in every direction.

Five minutes.

I stood at the corner and bounced up and down on the balls of my feet, waiting for the light to change and the walk signal to appear. Four minutes. Sweat was beginning to drip down my neck, even though the day was still cool. I'd been so confident when I hung up the phone with Julia, but now I had no idea what I was doing.

Even if I did find Ernest, what was I going to say to him? I could hope the words would come to me as they had with Julia—a fictional story spilling out of my mouth unprompted—but I had my doubts. Still, I searched for him. When the light finally changed, I practically sprinted across the street, finding comfort in the size of the crowd crossing the road. If a taxi wanted to run me over, it would have to take out twenty other pedestrians, as well.

I passed a small West End grocery store, a sub shop, and a pizza place. I walked by a hot dog stand and a small family of tourists on a motorized scooter tour of the city. As soon as

I'd moved to New York after college, I felt right at home. I liked the constant sound and the way the city truly never slept. There were always people out on the streets, heading to shops or theater shows or museums. But now I just wanted everything to freeze. To stop. I needed a pause button for life.

Two minutes.

Even though I tried not to, I found myself counting off the seconds as they passed, knowing my window was closing. Fifty-five. Fifty-four. Fifty-three.

A woman walked out of a laundromat to my left with a white basket full of folded clothes under one arm and a curly-haired toddler clinging to her hand. I side-stepped and started walking faster to try and get around them, but the little girl pulled on the woman's hand, stretching her arm out like a barrier while she reached for a bundle of balloons tied to the end of a newspaper cart.

"Mommy, please," she begged, jumping up and down. "Can I have one?"

Over the little girl's red hair and grinning face, I saw him.

Ernest Adrian was parked between two other taxis on the side of the road. Even with the sun glaring off the windshield, I could see enough of his dark beard to know it was him. Plus, I could easily double check his identity with the cab number Billy had sent me. It was him. He was right in front of me.

I jockeyed back and forth, trying to find a way around the now screaming toddler and the mother trying to balance her daughter and laundry, but they were taking up the whole sidewalk.

"Excuse me," I said desperately, though my words were lost in the cries of the toddler.

"MOMMY PLEASE!" The little girl had surprisingly good lungs for being so small.

"Excuse me," I said a bit louder, though I realized now it was useless.

I had one-minute left, if any time at all, and Ernest was still half a block away. Setting aside all decorum, I placed a hand on the shoulder of the already over-burdened mother and moved her to the right slightly, so I could squeeze between her and the buildings on the left. She spun around and gave me a dirty look as I passed, but I kept moving.

Ernest wiped his beard with his hands, and I watched him check his sideview mirrors, making sure no oncoming traffic was coming. I began to run, but I knew it was useless before I even started. The light of his taxi flicked on, and in one fluid motion, Ernest pulled away from the curb and merged in with the traffic.

I began waving my arm, thinking I could hail him, but he didn't stop. He drove to the end of the block and took a right back towards the sushi restaurant where Tucker was waiting for me. I'd missed him.

15

W hen I got back to the restaurant, Tucker was sitting at the table with his hands folded in front of him, a disappointed look on his usually good-natured face.

"Sorry about that," I said quietly, dropping down into the chair across from him. The walk back had been a slow and dejected one, so it had been twenty-five minutes since I'd first left the restaurant.

"Sorry about what?" Tucker asked. "What happened? You've been gone forever. The waitress brought me two flavored lemonades 'cause she thought I'd been stood up."

"Well, that's a bonus," I said, trying to smile.

Tucker shook his head. "You've been so strange this whole trip. We're always splittin' up and goin' our separate ways. I thought you were gonna be my tour guide, but I've been fendin' for myself. I just ordered us both sushi, even though I have no idea what most of it even is."

I wanted to tell Tucker that I had never offered to be his tour guide. He had invited himself on this trip and assumed I didn't mind. I'd wanted to do this alone. But I knew it wouldn't make any difference now. It would only serve to ruin whatever tenuous kind of friendship we had between us.

"I'm sorry, Tucker. I just—"

His phone rang. He pulled it out and then held up a finger to me as he answered it. I could tell immediately it was a business call of some kind. He had on his deep, work voice. The one that always made Suzy giggle like a high schooler. I missed Suzy. And Billy. I was beginning to regret having come to New York at all.

"Are ya sure?" Tucker asked. He glanced at me and then away quickly, looking suspicious. "Okay. Yes, of course. I won't tell anyone. Thanks a lot."

He hung up the phone and then folded his hands in his lap.

We sat in silence for a few seconds before I couldn't stand it any longer. "Who was that?"

"A police officer," he said.

"From Hillbilly Hollow? Is everything okay?"

"From here," he said. "From New York."

"Oh." I wrinkled my forehead. "I didn't realize you knew anyone from here."

"I didn't," he said, taking a deep breath as though he was about to unburden himself. "While you were off doin' your own things these past couple days, I was doin' my own thing, too. I contacted a few local officers, especially the ones who responded to the dead body inside your apartment building."

"You mean Blanche?"

He nodded. "I just wanted to be kept updated on their findings. I explained that I was a fellow officer and I had a good friend livin' in the building, so if there was any sign of foul play, I'd like to know."

"Okay," I said, eyes wide and urging, begging him to continue. "What was the call about?"

Tucker looked around and then leaned forward, his voice low. "None of this information can get out 'cause it could deter the investigation, but the medical examiner just finished Blanche's autopsy, and she discovered Blanche was poisoned."

I gasped. "Poison?"

He held a finger to his lips. "Yeah. Lots of it, too. Well beyond the lethal amount. Whoever did it really wanted her dead."

I quickly cycled back through the suspects I'd gathered since being in the city. Jay Wilkins had some very serious mommy issues, and enough anti-social tendencies to make him seem capable of something so heartless. Stephen Becket had motive, considering Blanche had been black-mailing him. And based on the vague threat he'd issued me as I'd left his apartment, he also had the temperament. And then there was Mable Abernathy. The fact that she was always giving away her baked treats made her pop into my head right away. But her only possible motive for the poisoning would be that Blanche had discussed trying to have her evicted, and I had no proof that had ever been made known to Mable, so it was a pretty tenuous thread.

And those were only the people I'd talked to since being back. All three had a potential motive. Based on those odds, every person living within the apartment building had a reason to kill Blanche. After all, she had never been the nicest woman.

"Is there any possibility of suicide?" I asked.

Tucker shrugged. "Sure, there always is. But I doubt it."

I doubted it, too. If Blanche had committed suicide, why would she be following me all over the country? The ghosts who visited me always wanted justice, but there was no need to solve Blanche's murder if she wasn't murdered.

We ate quietly, both of us deep in thought. Or, on Tucker's part, he may have been deep in frustration. Even though it wasn't entirely my fault, he was right when he said I'd been treating him a bit badly on the trip.

He had ordered a sushi platter while I'd been gone, allowing him to sample the main staples of the restaurant. After his first California roll, his face puckered in disgust. By the time he made it to the ahi tuna nigiri, he looked green.

"Are you doing okay?" I asked, sliding his water closer to him.

He took a deep drink and shook his head. "I'm not so sure this sushi stuff is for me."

"Let's get the check, then," I said, waving down the waitress. "I saw a hotdog vendor a few blocks back. A dog with everything on it will have you feeling better in no time."

He looked uncertain but agreed anyway. I paid the check, despite Tucker's feeble attempts to take it away from me, and then led him outside to the curb. As soon as the Autumn air hit him, he seemed to get some of his color back.

"I know you meant it as kind of a bad thing earlier, but I'll eat the fish at the Hillbilly Hollow Catfish Fry everyday for the rest of my life before I eat another sushi roll."

I laughed. "I love the yearly catfish fry! It's definitely not a bad thing."

Tucker watched with rapt attention as the vendor prepared his hotdog, complete with a spicy brown mustard and sauerkraut. He handed it to Tucker, who took a large bite almost immediately. I was moments away from ordering the same thing for myself when I looked to the curb and had to blink twice.

It was Ernest Adrian. He was parked just outside of a small theater, probably waiting for people to come pouring out after a show. I turned away quickly, hiding my face. If he saw me, he'd drive away the same way he had at the airport. He'd run. If I wanted to make the most of this opportunity fate had provided, it would have to be fast.

"Did you want anything?" Tucker asked, his brows pulled together in a question.

"No, I'm fine," I said, waving him away. I glanced back over my shoulder to be sure Ernest was still there. A few people walked out of the theater, and I knew I didn't have much time. Pretty soon, someone else would jump in his car and he'd be gone. It had to be now.

"Let's get a cab," I said, grabbing Tucker's arm.

"Or we could walk around a bit," he said, looking up to see the buildings and admire the architecture.

"I'm tired." Before he could protest anymore, I grabbed his arm, causing him to lose some of his sauerkraut to the concrete, and dragged him towards the curb. Halfway there, he stopped fighting and gave in.

Ernest looked up and saw us walking towards his cab, but since he didn't drive away I knew he didn't recognize me. I pulled open the back door, pushed Tucker in before me, and then slid in after him.

"Where to?" the cabbie asked, pulling away from the curb.

I almost gave my address but stopped short and instead told him to go to Matteo's.

Tucker took another bite of his hotdog. "You want pizza?"

I hummed an assent and stared down at the floor, not sure how I wanted to handle this.

"Are you okay, Emma?" Tucker asked. "Are you gonna be sick?"

"There's a cleaning fee if you get sick," Ernest said. "I can pull over."

"I'm fine," I said, still staring at the floor.

"I'm pulling over," Ernest said.

"No, don't!" The words came out as a command and both men looked at me. I could see Ernest's thick dark eyebrows in the rearview mirror. They were raised in surprise, and the longer he looked at me, the more they began to furrow. Finally, I saw his entire face go slack in shock.

"You," he whispered.

"Hi." I felt stupid for offering a greeting to the man who had changed my life, perhaps forever, with his reckless driving, but I didn't know what else to say.

"You two know each other?" Tucker asked, looking back and forth from me to Ernest and back again.

I nodded. "In a way."

"What are you doing here?" Ernest asked. "Why are you here? How did you find me?"

"It doesn't matter," I said. I didn't want Julia to get in trouble for giving away Ernest's location, and I also didn't want to burn that particular bridge in case I needed to use it again.

"It matters to me," he roared. "What is this? Some kind of sting operation?"

Tucker had forgotten all about the last few bites of his hotdog now, and was sitting straight up, on high alert. "Sting operation? What's he talking about, Emma?"

I took a deep, steadying breath. "I was in an accident a few months back. A cab hit me in an intersection and then fled the scene. They never found him."

Tucker nodded, waiting for me to continue.

I flicked my eyes towards Ernest in the front seat, and Tucker's mouth fell open. "You hit her and drove away? Do you realize that's against the law?"

"I'm sure he realizes, Tucker," I said.

"We need to call the local police." Tucker pulled out his phone. I noticed Ernest stiffen and the car swerved slightly. I grabbed the phone and shoved it under my leg.

"I don't want to call the police."

"Emma—" Tucker began.

I shook my head. "No. I just want to talk to him." I shifted my focus to Ernest. "I just want to talk to you."

"About what?" he asked. "I have nothing to say."

"Well, I do," I said, realizing how true it was. I hadn't talked much about the accident since it had happened, and suddenly I felt prepared to rehash everything. "The accident may have ended for you when you drove away, but it has changed my entire life. I suffered a major head injury. I've been going to therapy to deal with visions and hallucinations"—I decided not to mention that I now believed the visions to be actual ghosts, because I didn't want Ernest or Tucker to think I was crazy—"and I had to move out of the city to be with family while I recovered."

"That's why you came back?" Tucker asked.

Ernest's head lowered so I could no longer see his eyes in the rearview mirror. I had no idea what he was thinking, but the fact that he was still driving and not pulling over had to be a good thing.

"I'm afraid of walking through the city now. I have nightmares of the accident. I don't blame you for hitting me, but I blame you for driving away. You should have stayed."

"I would lose my job," he said finally, his voice breaking

around the words. "I had official warnings on record. I could have gone to jail."

"You *should* go to jail," Tucker said, making Ernest jump.

"Did you ever think about it, at least?" I asked. "Did you wonder what happened to me?"

He nodded. "Yes. I wondered, but I was too afraid to check the papers or public record. I was afraid I'd hear that you were dead, and I'd never be able to live with myself. I've barely been able to live with myself as it is. I see you everywhere. I just keep waiting for the police to figure out it was me and come looking. It's been torture."

In that moment, I realized I'd made the right decision. For months, the driver in the cab had been a monster to me. A man with no feelings or remorse who had run me down in the street and then peeled away from the scene laughing. It was nice to know that hadn't been the case. He had simply panicked, and he'd made a terrible decision.

"I'm sorry the past few months have been tough on you," I said.

Tucker snapped his head towards me. "You're apologizing to him? He hit you, Emma."

"Please don't apologize to me," Ernest said. "I don't deserve it. I'm sorry I ran away. I'm sorry I didn't stop to make sure you were okay." There was a long pause, and then his voice came out soft and uncertain. "Will you have any permanent damage from the head injury?"

"My doctor doesn't know yet," I said. "It's likely."

Ernest shook his head and let out a shaky sigh. "I'm so sorry. I will never forgive myself."

I'd dreamt about this moment for months—meeting the man who had hit me and making him feel the pain and torment I'd experienced. But now, watching him suffer, I realized how little joy I was getting from it. In fact, instead of joy, there was sympathy and frustration. I didn't want to be part of a chain of unhappiness.

"That isn't what I want. Maybe if you turned yourself in and faced the consequences, you could find some relief." I thought of the way I'd run home to Missouri to try and escape the visions I was having. Being in a new place, away from the memories of the accident felt good at first, but it didn't last. The visions returned, and the anxiety that came along with them didn't go away until I faced them head on. Until I accepted them for what they were—spirits.

His mouth twisted to the side, unsure. "Maybe."

"Just consider it," I said. "I won't press charges."

"Emma, what are you saying?" Tucker asked.

I gave him a sharp look and shook my head. He pinched his lips together and looked out the window, practically vibrating with frustration. It was clear that as a police officer, the idea that I was going to let this man walk away did not sit well with him.

"You can pull over here," I said, pointing towards the side of the road. "You don't need to take us all the way back to Brooklyn."

Ernest pulled over without arguing, probably as anxious to get me out of his cab as I was to get out.

"I am sorry," he said, turning around to look at me, face to face for the first time.

All things considered, he looked like a nice man.

"Thank you," I said. "Me too."

———

16

Tucker didn't say a word as I found us another cab and we drove the remaining fifteen minutes back to my apartment. It was very unlike him. Usually, he would be pointing at things through the window and asking me if I'd ever eaten at any of the thirty restaurants we passed. I'd spent most of our trip wishing he would just leave me alone, but now the silence was unnerving.

When the car pulled up in front of my apartment, I paid the fare and slid out, the dress for Annie's wedding draped over my arm.

"Could you wait here for a second?" Tucker asked the driver. "I'll be right back."

He got out of the car and stood in front of me, arms crossed over his chest, jaw clenched.

"I'm sorry about that," I started to say, but Tucker held up a hand.

"I don't even know what *that* was, but there's obviously a lot about this trip that you didn't tell me," he said. "I've been here for you every step of the way. I'm a Sheriff, for good-ness' sake. I could've helped you track that man down. I could've helped you confront him. But instead, you sprung the whole thing on me."

My face flushed with embarrassment and shame. Tucker was right. I'd excluded him even when he could have been an asset to me.

"I came on this trip, because...I don't know," Tucker said with a shrug. "I guess I thought maybe there could be some-thin' here between us, but it's obvious you don't respect me or my position."

"That isn't it," I said, eager to jump in. "I just didn't know how to explain everything. It felt too complicated. I didn't know if you'd understand."

That was only partially true. I knew how to explain everything. I'd told Billy without any trouble. It all just felt too personal for Tucker.

"I'm not dumb, Emma. I can understand plenty of things," he said.

Another rumble of shame moved through me. Suzy and I had long whispered behind his back that Tucker was dumber than a box of rocks. And as true as it was, it still wasn't kind to say.

"Sure, you're not, Tucker. I know that. It's just—"

"It's just that you'd rather keep yer secrets and stick close to yer friends and refuse to let in anyone new," he said, rotating away from me, looking off down the road, his eyes narrowed. "I should've seen that. Maybe I am dumb for thinking you'd ever think of me over him."

"Who?"

"You aren't dumb, either," Tucker said, pursing his lips. When I still didn't respond, he shook his head. "Billy. I was talkin' about Billy."

What was with everyone pushing me and Billy together?

Why couldn't a man and a woman just be friends without people getting other ideas?

The driver of the taxi honked his horn even though we were only standing a few feet away. Tucker waved to him and turned back to me. "It doesn't matter. I just wanted to let you know I'm gonna head home tonight. Or as soon as I can get a flight back."

"Tucker," I said softly, torn between feeling relieved and guilty.

He opened the door and shook his head. "Thanks for being my tour guide around the city. I'll see you back in Hillbilly Hollow."

Before I could say anything else, he ducked into the backseat and the cab drove away.

On one hand, Tucker's romantic interest had finally been dealt with. But on the other hand, I felt terrible and I didn't understand it. Tucker had never been one of my close friends. He had never been a major part of my life, either before I left Missouri for college or after I'd returned. So why did his obvious disappointment in me bother me so much?

As I turned back towards the building, a flash of blue caught my eye. Instantly, my body reacted. My heart rate increased, and my breath caught in my throat. Seeing things move along the edges of my vision used to be the result of an overactive imagination, but now it was because of an overactive spirit world. However, when I looked towards the movement, I only saw a bright blue bird perched on the edge of a feeder dish, and my shoulders relaxed.

Mable kept a small array of animal feeders outside of her first-floor window. There was a hummingbird feeder on a metal pole that she filled with a sugar liquid, a hanging bowl of bird seed, and a small wooden box with a hole in the side just large enough for a squirrel to stick its arm through. The feeders were Mable's way of connecting with an outside world that she no longer entered. If she didn't want to go out into nature, she would bring it to her.

The blue bird—a welcome sight among the thousands of pigeons I saw in the city everyday—hopped along the edge of the bowl, tipping forward and rooting through the bowl of seed, spilling some over the side and onto the ground. It extended its vibrant wings for a second as it glided down to the ground and began pecking at the fallen seeds. The sight was so familiar to me that I smiled. When I was little, Grandma and I would spread feed for the chickens and then watch as they all squawked around and pecked at their dinner. Even as a teenager, when I began to resent the small-town charm of Hillbilly Hollow, I still loved to go out with Grandma or Grandpa in the morning and feed the animals.

Standing there, watching the bird, I realized how much I missed Hillbilly Hollow. How much I missed the farm I'd grown up on and seeing my grandparents regularly. Being away from home for so many years, I'd been able to forget why I loved it so much. But after having spent a few months back there with my family and friends and the farm, I was beginning to realize that the middle of nowhere, Missouri was home to me. My grandparents and Suzy and Billy were my home. They always had been, and I couldn't wait to get back.

The bird was still picking up the seeds when I climbed the stairs and closed the door softly behind me, hoping the slamming wouldn't scare the hungry critter away.

17

I paused in front of the basement stairs for a moment, contemplating going back up to my apartment and lying down for a while. I'd taken the three flights of stairs two at a time and hung my dress up in the coat closet behind the door before closing it and going immediately back to the lobby. It was the middle of the afternoon, but it felt like I'd been awake for three days straight. My eyes burned, and my legs felt heavy. But the information Tucker had passed along at lunch pestered me, like a continuous tap on the shoulder, pushing me onward. Blanche had been poisoned.

The hallway that led to Jay Wilkins' apartment seemed even darker than it had the last time I'd walked it. The walls seemed to be pressing in on me, growing more and more narrow the further I walked. Halfway down, I contemplated turning back. It was a longshot that Jay would even talk to me again. After I'd bombarded him with questions the first time and then had my sheriff friend show up at his door, he probably wouldn't be too excited to see my face. Though, I didn't imagine Jay was ever too excited to see many people's faces.

Still, I knocked, and Jay answered after the second one. He flung the door open, eyes wide as if he was expecting someone. When he saw it was me, his shoulders drooped in disappointment and he sagged against the door frame.

"Oh. Hi."

"Hi," I said, trying to sound marginally more cheerful than he had.

"If you're here about the window, Paul said he took care of it this morning," Jay said.

I furrowed my brow in confusion before remembering my leaky window, which I was almost positive Paul had not fixed simply because he had been unable to fix it the previous five times he'd tried. "Right, yes. I'm sure he did great."

"Then why are you here?" he asked suspiciously.

I leaned forward and lowered my voice. "I heard from a reliable source that your mother's death has been ruled a poisoning."

Tucker had told me to keep it quiet, but I had to assume that even if Jay was a suspect in the murder of his mother, the police would have told him the results of her autopsy. If they had, then I did nothing wrong by repeating the information. If they hadn't, I could gauge his reaction to see whether I considered him a suspect.

Jay's expression didn't change at all, but suddenly, he stepped towards me, closing the distance between us, and whispered harshly. "Have you told anyone else?"

"No, no," I said, too surprised to say anything else.

"Keep it that way," he said. "That is the last thing I need getting out. The tenants would panic."

"Why would they panic?" I asked. "Do you think there's a serial killer on the loose or something?"

"What? No," he said, scrunching up his nose like he thought I was crazy. "I don't need them to think rat poison will find its way into their food, too."

I gasped. "Rat poison?"

Jay seemed to realize what he'd let slip and took a deep breath. "I have an inspector looking at the building now. I'm actually waiting on the results. But there are no rats. We've never had a problem with rats. I've searched the maintenance closets and my mom's apartment several times and haven't found any rat poison. I have no idea how she came into contact with enough of it to kill her. Her cat eats almost everything she eats, and the cat isn't dead, so it isn't just lying around. I don't know."

Jay's face reddened the longer he spoke, and his breathing was growing more and more labored. I wanted to ask him many more questions, but I was growing a little worried that he'd pass out. He looked overwhelmed, which seemed appropriate considering everything he'd dealt with in the preceding days.

"Your mom had a cat?"

He looked at me like he wasn't sure he'd heard me correctly, but then he slowly nodded his head. "Yeah, she had a cat."

"What happened to it?" Jay's apartment showed no signs of a new furry roommate.

"It's still in her apartment," he said with a shrug.

"By itself?"

"I'm allergic," he said.

My animal loving heart shattered. Poor kitty. How long had it been in the apartment alone?

"I go up and feed it twice a day, so it's fine," he said.

That settled it. I'd already accepted that I wouldn't get much more information out of Jay Wilkins and would have to find answers myself but hearing about Blanche's lonely cat solidified a plan in my mind. I'd break into her apartment to conduct a search of my own, and then take the cat with me.

18

With foul play suspected in Blanche's murder, I had to be especially careful about breaking into her apartment. Not only did I not want to disrupt anything that could be a clue, I didn't want to leave any new ones that would point investigators towards me rather than the true killer. Also, I didn't need anyone—mostly Mable—seeing me sneak into the dead woman's apartment. As nice as Mable was—assuming she wasn't the murderer—I had no doubt she wouldn't hesitate to turn me into the police for breaking and entering.

I opened the door from the basement stairs to the lobby as quietly as possible, letting it gently click back into place behind me, and then crossed the lobby, sticking as close to the wall as possible. When I got to Blanche's door, I slid my debit card along the crack in the door and felt the locking mechanism shift and then release.

One of my most enduring complaints about the apartment building—aside from my leaking window—had always been security. The ancient and inefficient locks could be picked with nothing more than an envelope or a credit card. It was why I'd installed my own deadbolt in my door, despite Blanche warning me I would have to pay for the "damages" to the door when I moved out. That was fine. I'd told her I would pay for an entirely new door if it meant I wouldn't have to worry about anyone breaking into my apartment.

As I closed Blanche's door behind me, I wondered whether someone hadn't broken into her apartment before she died. They could have snuck in and poisoned something in her fridge. Or, more horrifically, they could have force fed her the poison. I shuddered at the thought, and then pushed it away. There was no sense in dwelling on something that might not have even happened.

The room felt stale and oddly warm, despite the chill in the air outside. I didn't see any sign of the cat as I moved into the living room that looked remarkably like mine, except Blanche's furniture was at least ten years older and covered in a floral pattern. But as soon as I moved into the hallway, the strong scent of ammonia hit me. I covered my nose.

"Here, Kitty Kitty," I said in a nasally voice.

I could see the litter box through the open bedroom door at the end of the small hallway, but there was still no sign of the cat. I froze, trying to listen for any rustle of movement. I was even holding my breath, so when my phone vibrated in my back pocket, the surprise of it made me yelp and lurch forward a step. As soon as I did, the shuttered doors covering the washer and dryer to my right burst open as a black streak of fur shot out from between them with a yowl.

Whatever air was left in me came out in a whoosh as I slammed back against the hallway wall, hand pressed to my heart, trying to bring the rhythm back to normal. When I felt prepared, I stepped away from the wall and moved slowly back towards the living room. The cat was lying on its side on the living room floor, paws extended. It looked submissive, but I knew better. Cats lay on their sides to better showcase their claws. Blanche's cat was simply showing me her weapons. I turned my body away from her, letting her know I wasn't a threat, and then stood still. My phone vibrated again, but I ignored it. It was probably Billy checking in on me since he'd given me the information about Ernest a couple hours before and hadn't heard anything from me yet.

Slowly, over the next few minutes, I worked my way closer to the cat, who had shifted from a defensive position to a seated one and finally to lying down with its head on its paws (gender was still a mystery). When I dared to reach out and pet the cat, not only did it nuzzle its head into my palm, but it purred. Sweet success.

Jay said he was feeding the cat, but the food and water bowls were both empty. I found some dry cat food in the pantry and ran cool water from the tap, and the cat ate and drank like it had been days since its last meal. My heart broke. Its owner had died, and then no one had cared enough to properly take care of the animal. It was one-hundred percent decided. I would definitely be taking the no-name, mysterious gendered cat home to Missouri with me.

While the cat ate, I poked around Blanche's kitchen very carefully. Jay had been in and out of his mother's apartment a few times since her death, at least, and he was still alive. So, my fear of secondhand poisoning was slim, but it was better to be safe than sorry. There were a few less than fresh items in the fridge and a moldy loaf of bread in the pantry. Otherwise, everything seemed okay. The trash can under her sink stunk to high heavens, but a little bit of poking through the rubbish didn't reveal anything sinister. Just a discarded pound of hamburger—the source of the smell, no doubt—a spoiled bag of spinach, and a paper plate and some plastic wrap. Normal. Completely normal.

I closed the cabinet, ignoring the very strong urge I felt to take Blanche's trash to the dumpster. I didn't need Jay coming back and growing suspicious that someone had been in the apartment. Though, based on the fact that the cat had been near dehydration and the trash can was full of rot, he probably wouldn't have noticed if I'd decided to clean up the place a little bit.

I wondered where in the apartment Blanche had been found. Jay hadn't offered up the information, and I hadn't wanted to ask. It felt personal. However, not knowing made every step in Blanche's apartment give me the feeling that I was walking over a headstone in a cemetery. I felt like I was disrespecting her in some way. Had she collapsed in the kitchen after ingesting whatever poisoned item she had been given? Or had she managed to make it to the living room and drop onto her sofa before succumbing? The obvious dent in the middle of the sofa suddenly took on a more ominous meaning. I blinked a few times to clear the mental picture my mind was drawing and turned away.

The cat had finished eating and was grooming itself in the middle of the living room floor, licking its paws and then batting at its face. When properly taken care of, the animal was clearly very docile. He or she would probably make a great friend for Snowball. I smiled to myself, thinking what my grandpa would say when he found out I was going to be sleeping in the attic with a cat in addition to a goat. I shook my head. My life sure had changed in the past few months.

My phone vibrated in my back pocket again and I

remembered the calls and texts from before. I pulled it out and, just as I'd expected, it was Billy.

"I'm fine," I said by way of a greeting. "Totally safe."

He sighed. "That's a relief. I spent the last few hours wondering whether I had sent you into the company of a crazy man. Did you find him?"

"I did." It was crazy how busy the day had been. So many things had happened that I'd nearly forgotten about talking to Ernest.

"And?" he asked. "How did it go?"

I thought about it for a minute, trying to decide if it went the way I'd hoped. And really, it hadn't. Before meeting him, I'd hoped Ernest would scream and yell at me. I'd hoped he would threaten me so I could call the police and have him arrested. But instead, he had been upset. Apologetic, even.

"It went really well," I said.

There was a long pause. "You're eventually going to elaborate, aren't you? Because you're giving me nothing here."

I laughed. "Yes, I'll tell you everything over shakes at the diner."

"Good. Because as I've said, you owe me."

"I do. I owe you big, Billy."

There was a long silence where I wasn't sure Billy was going to respond. The quiet between us felt loaded for some reason. Then, he let out a breath. "Well, thanks for letting me know you were okay."

"Of course," I said. "Sorry it took me so long to respond to your texts."

"What?" he asked.

"You called and texted earlier, but I was in the middle of taming a half-feral cat."

"Okay, add that to the list of things you'll need to explain to me when you get back to Hillbilly Hollow," he said with a laugh. "But I only called you the one time. You answered right away."

"Oh," I said, brow furrowed. Then who had been calling me? "Okay. I have to get going, but I'll let you know when my flight is."

"See you soon, Emma."

As soon as the phone beeped to signal the end of the call, I pulled down my notifications bar and saw that I had three missed texts and a call from Tucker. When we'd talked less than an hour before, he had been dead set on leaving New York City as soon as possible. I wondered if things had changed.

TUCKER: I'm sorry about what I said. I'm coming back to sort this out. Can you let me in?

TUCKER: I'm outside now.

TUCKER: Are you mad at me or are you not seeing these messages?

TUCKER HAD SENT the messages only fifteen minutes before, but he could have already grown tired of waiting and left. Still, even if I wasn't interested in Tucker romantically, I didn't like the way we'd left things. We needed to talk.

The cat was still grooming itself, and I suspected it would be for the next hour at least. So, I gave it a quick scratch behind the ears, which earned me a contented purr, and then slipped out of Blanche's apartment as quietly as I'd entered. I couldn't lock the door behind me since I didn't have the key, but I just had to hope Jay would blame the open door on the building's faulty locks. Perhaps it would encourage him to update them.

I couldn't see Tucker through the glass front door of the building, and there was no sign of him anywhere when I walked outside and looked up and down the block.

I called him and then pressed the phone into my ear, hoping he'd pick up. I wasn't sure I wanted to tell him about breaking into Blanche's apartment. Even though we'd just had a conversation about me lying to him, it didn't change the fact that he was a police officer and I'd technically broken the law by going into Blanche's apartment. Not to mention, I'd potentially contaminated a crime scene. The last thing I needed was my local Sheriff thinking I was a criminal. The phone rang five times before his voicemail picked up.

"Hey Tucker, it's Emma. Sorry I didn't see your call and texts before. I don't want you to think I was ignoring you. If you're still close by, come back and we can talk."

As I hung up and turned around, I noticed something lying on the dirt beneath Mable's shuttered window. At first it looked like a blue and white tennis ball or something, but when I moved closer, I could see the tiny orange feet coming from the bottom. It was the bluebird I'd seen eating from Mable's bird feeder when Tucker and I had come back from talking to Ernest. But now, it was dead.

I tip-toed towards the bird's corpse, still afraid it was only stunned and would wake any moment, flapping off and scaring me half to death in the process. But the only movement coming from the body was the flutter of feathers in the light Autumn wind.

How had this happened? I'd seen the bird an hour ago and it looked as alive as could be. I walked around to the side, so I could get a look at its face and beak. There was no sign of the bird having smacked into one of the building's windows or any other deadly trauma. It had simply...

dropped dead. Much like the bird Tucker and I had seen lying on the front steps of the apartment building two days before, this bird was a perfect specimen, aside from the fact that its heart had stopped beating.

A shiver ran down my spine, and I was becoming well versed enough in supernatural activity to recognize it as the chill brought on by a nearby ghost. I spun around expecting to see Blanche, but she wasn't there.

"Blanche?" I whispered. "Was that you?"

Still no sign of her, but I could have sworn I just saw my breath in the air. Something strange was happening, and I didn't understand it. Was Blanche trying to send me a sign, or had a low-pressure storm front suddenly moved through my block?

I pulled out my phone and called Tucker again, mostly because I wanted to hear another human voice. It rang once and then twice, and I prayed Tucker would pick up. Just then, a wind whipped down the street, swirling my hair around my face and making me drop my phone. I yelped in surprise and tried to get my hair out of my eyes and mouth. As I did, though, I realized that even though my phone was no longer pressed to my ear, I could still hear Tucker's phone ringing. Except, rather than coming from the speaker of my phone on the ground, the sound was coming from behind me.

I turned around and stepped towards the building, avoiding the dead bluebird. The closer I got to Mable's window, the louder Tucker's phone became. I tilted my head to the side and listened as his phone rang for the fifth and final time before going silent.

This time when I felt the chill down my back, I turned around and knew I'd find Blanche there. She was hovering above the sidewalk next to my dropped cell phone. Her lips were moving silently just as they had every time I'd seen her before, except this time there was something in her hand. Maybe she wasn't trying to talk after all.

"What is that?" I asked, pointing to the dark blob between her fingers. "Are you chewing something? What are you eating?"

Blanche's foggy shape lifted the dark square to her mouth and took a bite. Moments later, she seized, flickered, and disappeared.

Suddenly, the pieces of the puzzle I'd been holding clicked into place. Everything made sense.

Mable Abernathy had murdered Blanche.

19

Observations that had meant little to me at first glance now took on importance. There were plenty of clues pointing to Mable that I hadn't wanted to believe earlier. Why? Because Mable was nice, and, if I was being honest, old. Elderly people weren't murderers. Except, they were. Apparently.

I'd seen the blue bird eating from the seed outside of Mable's window only an hour before, and now it was dead. I'd seen another dead bird two days before. For whatever reason, Mable was poisoning the city's animals. But did that really mean she could do the same thing to Blanche?

In my mind's eye, I saw the paper plate and plastic wrap on the top of Blanche's rotting trash can. It was the same paper plate and plastic wrap that Mable had been handing out to me for years, the plate holding a variety of her baked goods—brownies, muffins, lemon squares. She didn't hand treats out to everyone who walked by her door, but she gave them to a lot of people, including Blanche.

How much rat poison had it taken to put Blanche down? The plate in the trash can was empty. Had it only been one brownie or had Blanche simply eaten them all in one sitting? Our landlady was not known for being ladylike or delicate. I wouldn't have put it past her to eat the whole plate by herself. Either way, though, Mable had poisoned the treats and handed them to Blanche, probably with a smile.

And now, she had Tucker's phone.

I stepped away from her window and picked up my phone from the sidewalk, trying not to think about what that meant for Tucker. What reason would Mable have had for hurting him? According to Jay, Blanche had been talking about getting Mable evicted so she could raise the rent on her unit, which seemed reason enough for the mildly agoraphobic woman to want Blanche dead. But Tucker was a stranger to her. A good guy without a mean bone in his entire body. What had happened between the time when he called me and when I'd finally come outside to meet him?

As I mounted the steps to the building and stepped into the lobby, I tried not to imagine the worst. Tucker was fine. He had to be. Still, there was no time to lose.

My hand was shaking as I knocked on Mable's door. Part of me felt silly for being so scared. Mable was an elderly woman. I could overpower her if anything went wrong. But another part of me knew I had to stay alert. Poison was a sneaky act of murder. I couldn't let Mable catch me off guard.

I heard a chain lock on the other side of the door slide open and then Mable's face appeared in the narrow crack of the door.

"Hello sweetheart," she said, her dry lips pulled into a smile.

If I hadn't been paying attention to the details, I might not have noticed anything out of the ordinary. But I was paying attention. Mable's smile didn't reach her eyes. Her chest was rising and falling faster than normal, air puffing from between her lips like she was struggling to catch her breath.

"Hi Mable," I said, trying to sound casual. "I'm going to be leaving again soon, and I just wanted to stop in and say goodbye."

"Oh," she said, mouth pulling into a frown. "That's too bad. It has been good to have you back. I'll have to send you home with a plate of goodies."

Yeah, right. There were two dead birds outside who showed me what eating Mable's goodies could do. Not to mention Blanche at the morgue. But I kept the thoughts to myself.

"Of course, that would be great."

Mable smiled and nodded, and then took a step back into her apartment, the door closing half an inch. "I'll have them ready for you in the morning. Just knock on the door before you leave."

I heard what sounded like a low moan from deep in the apartment, though it also could have been the wind whistling through the building's leaky windows or a footstep on the next floor. Mable turned back towards her living room, letting me know she'd heard the noise too. When she looked back at me, her face had gone pale.

"Are you feeling all right, Mable?" I asked, stepping forward and pressing a hand on her front door.

Mable stiffened and began to nod incessantly. "Oh yes. Perfectly fine. Don't worry about me. I'm old, but sturdy."

"Okay," I said hesitantly. "You just seem out of breath and pale. I would hate to leave you alone and then have something happen."

"I'm fine," she snapped. She followed the harsh words

with a smile. "Just tired and a little busy. I have some treats in the oven now actually. I ought to check on them. Goodbye dear."

The smell of treats baking in Mable's oven always wafted into the lobby. It was impossible not to know when she was baking something. But I didn't smell anything, and I was standing in front of her open door. Except, it wouldn't be open for long. Mable was stepping back and pushing it shut.

I had a split second to decide what to do. I could bring my suspicions to the police and hope they made it in time to save Tucker, who was likely inside Mable's apartment. Or, I could take matters into my own hands, trusting that I could overpower the small woman.

Mable's door was an inch from closing when I shoved my foot against the base of the door and threw my shoulder against the flimsy wood.

Mable cried out in surprise from the other side of the door, and I heard her stumble back. "What are you doing?"

As soon as the door was thrown wide, it became obvious why Mable had been trying to hurry me away. Sprawled across her plastic-covered floral sofa was Tucker. His head lolled to one side and his hands were limply flopped in his lap. If it hadn't been for the slow rising and falling of his chest, I would have been sure he was dead.

I ran across the room and knelt in front of him, grabbing his hands in mine. His fingers felt cold.

"Tucker." I shook his arms and reached up to pat his tan cheek. "What did you do to him, Mable?"

The old woman didn't answer, but I heard the door click shut.

Tucker's eyelids lifted slightly, and I could see his eyes rolling around, fighting to focus.

He tried to say my name, but it came out like a long sigh instead. "Mmmm-ha."

"I'm here," I said. "You're okay. Do you remember what happened?"

I lifted Tucker up by his shoulders, trying to get him to sit up straight, but as soon as I let go, he slid back down again.

"Ate sumting," he said, his tongue refusing to cooperate.

"What did you give him, Mable?" I asked. "Tell me now. Is he going to be okay?"

Mable was still near the front door, but her back was turned to me now and the closet door was open. Suddenly, she turned around and I saw the gun in her hand. It was a handgun, nothing flashy or showy, but it would get the job done. It would silence me and Tucker forever if I didn't do something to stop her.

"I have a feeling neither of you are going to be okay for much longer," Mable said, her bottom lip tucked beneath her top, her chin dimpled.

"Why are you doing this?" I asked. "Just let me take him out of here. Let me get him some help."

"He doesn't need help. He needs a nap," Mable said. "And you know why I'm doing this, don't you?"

I didn't answer. The less I said, the better. Mable was clearly unstable.

"You knocked on my door because you know what I've done," Mable said, her voice cracking. "And you are coming to undo my hard work. You came back to the city to wreck everything for me."

"You wrecked everything already," I said. "You killed Blanche."

Mable lifted her head up, the loose skin around her throat stretching. I could see that her arms were already shaking from the effort of holding the gun up, but that didn't mean she wouldn't pull the trigger. In fact, it meant she might pull it even sooner than she would have otherwise. "That may be true, but I had a good reason. I had a very good reason."

"She was going to evict you."

Mable nodded. "Blanche knew that I couldn't leave the apartment, but she didn't care. She only cared about money. Greed is a sin just like murder, isn't it? What I did to her wasn't any worse than what she was going to do to me. A sin is a sin. Plus, she didn't have any trouble taking baked goods from me even while she actively planned to evict me. She was a horrible woman."

"Evicting you would have been wrong," I said softly. "But you killed someone. You ended a life."

"And gluttony," Mable added, one finger in the air as if she'd just remembered something. "Gluttony killed her, too. There wasn't enough poison in any one slice of brownie to put someone as large as Blanche under. It took the whole plate. If she hadn't eaten them all so quickly, she may have survived and only experienced a stomach ache.

I remembered the empty plate in Blanche's trash. I didn't know how many brownies Mable gave her, but Blanche ate every single one. Apparently, Mable believed an affinity for sweets also deemed someone worthy of death. If that was the case, she should go ahead and shoot me now. Prior to learning Mable liked to add a deadly ingredient to her desserts, I used to eat her goodie plates in one afternoon.

"What did the birds do to deserve to die?" I asked, the words coming out in a grunt while I propped Tucker up against my side. I didn't want him to collapse forward and compromise his otherwise steady breathing.

Mable gave me a small smile, as though she was pleased

I had solved that part of the puzzle, as well. "Being inside as I am, it's nice to see some nature outside my window. I've always loved setting out bird seed and squirrel snacks, and they have always gone over very well with a large number of animals. But, recently, I noticed a few of the birds were eating more than their fair share. They were grotesque, fat birds that had no self-control."

"So, you poisoned them?" I asked.

She shook her head. "No, I laid a trap, and they fell into it. I put a very low dosage in the food—not enough to kill an animal if they only ate a small amount. But much like Blanche, a few of the birds didn't know when to quit. They did it to themselves."

I wanted to tell Mable that her logic was flawed. If it hadn't been for the poison she added to the food, Blanche and the birds would simply be a little heavier. Instead, they were dead. And the only person at fault was Mable.

"What did Tucker do to deserve this?" I asked.

Mable looked at Tucker and tilted her head to the side, her yellowing eyes thoughtful. "I noticed you snooping around as soon as you got back in the building. I thought maybe you'd let it go, but you kept talking to Jay, and then I saw you going into Blanche's room this afternoon. Not to mention, you brought your own personal officer back with you."

"He's just a friend," I argued. "He isn't here as an officer. He didn't know I was investigating Blanche's murder."

Mable didn't seem to hear me. Or, if she did, she ignored it. "Why would the two of you care about the death of a woman you barely knew anyway? She was your landlady, but you and I both know she wasn't a nice woman. Why did it concern you so much?"

I wasn't about to tell Mable that I'd been seeing spirits.

First of all, the information was personal and sensitive. Second, there was a good chance Mable would think I was crazy, which would be just another reason for her to shoot me.

"It doesn't matter," Mable continued. "I knew you were looking into Blanche's death, and when your friend showed up at my door looking for you, I saw my chance to put all of this to rest once and for all. I'd take care of him first and then lure you here and do the same to you. One at a time would have been easier, but I'm adaptable. You don't get to be as old as I am without being able to adjust."

"How are you going to take care of us?" I asked, genuinely curious. "What do you plan to do with our bodies?"

"Do you really want to spoil the entire plan?" Mable asked, exasperated. "I think the time for questions is over. Lift him up," she said, using the gun to gesture to Tucker. Her hand was shaking more noticeably now, and I worried she'd pull the trigger by accident.

Tucker's body was already leaning into mine, so I grabbed his arm and threw it around my shoulder, standing up slowly. Immediately, my thighs began to shake under his weight. He groaned and tried to open his eyes, but they stayed shut.

"Onto the fire escape," Mable said, her voice now shaking like her arm.

"Mable," I said, trying to engage her humanity. "You don't have to do this. You can't get away with it."

"You don't know that," she said quickly, cutting me off. "Onto the fire escape or I'll shoot you. Poison is my preference, but I will shoot."

Mable looked unsteady, and I wanted to try and wrestle the gun away from her, but I had Tucker to think about. He

couldn't defend himself in his current state. If I made a
single wrong move, he could end up hurt or worse. So, I
decided to take my chance with the fire escape.

I leaned Tucker against the window frame as I kicked
my leg over and then stepped out onto the rickety metal
staircase. Tucker was almost unconscious but had enough
wherewithal to reach for my hand. I pulled him onto the
stairs.

"Up," Mable ordered from inside the apartment. "And if
you even think about knocking on any windows for help,
I'll shoot."

"I don't know if I can make it all the way to the top. He's
heavy," I said.

Mable shrugged. "If you both fall then that makes my
job even easier. Up."

She wagged the gun at me again, reminding me she still
had the power, as if I could have possibly forgotten. I gritted
my teeth, and stair by stair, lugged Tucker up the stairs. He
moved his feet slightly, dragging them across the metal, and
placed one hand on the railing. But the little help he offered
was hardly enough to make a difference.

I turned back several times to see if Mable was following
us, but she wasn't yet. I realized then why she may have
been shaking so much the closer she got to the window—
Mable was scared to leave her apartment. In that moment,
hope surged in my chest that Mable's fears would incapaci-
tate her. That she would be frozen in terror, unable to follow
after us and see her plan through to the end. However, the
next time I turned around, I saw the old woman cautiously
climbing out of her window. Then, she began a slow and
steady trek up to the roof.

If I hadn't been forced to deal with Tucker's weight, I
would have sprinted up the stairs and then found a way

back into the building from the roof, hoping I could dodge whatever shots Mable would aim at me from such a long distance. However, Tucker made that impossible. We were moving so slowly up the stairs that Mable was actually gaining on us. By the time Tucker and I made it to the top, landing in a heaving heap on the asphalt roof, Mable was only ten steps below us.

She appeared on the edge of the roof with a small snack bag in her hands. She tossed it at me, the bag landing a foot away.

"Enjoy," she said with a fake smile.

The bag contained two brownie squares—broken and crumbling from Mable's throw, but otherwise delicious looking. It was almost unfair how good they looked. The tops were a perfect, crackled brown crust, and the inside was shiny and gooey. If Mable had handed me these same brownies on a plate like she always did as I walked through the lobby, I would have eaten them both just like Blanche had. I would have enjoyed them.

"No," I said, kicking the bag further away and then standing up.

Mable sighed. "This is the easiest way. It will be better for you this way. A little discomfort and then nothing. Much preferable to a gunshot."

I shook my head. "I won't kill myself for you."

"Mmmm-ha," Tucker mumbled, reaching for my hand.

"Your friend is beginning to resurface, I believe," Mable said, pointing the still-shaking gun at him. "It would be kinder of me to shoot him now. He wouldn't even feel it."

I spun myself to cover Tucker, as if Mable wouldn't shoot me just as callously as she would Tucker. "You don't have to do this. It won't work, anyway. People will still find out."

Mable shrugged her thin shoulders. "Maybe. But there

will be doubts. I'll tell the police how Blanche tried to raise your rent while you were gone and how angry it made you. I'll tell them how you anonymously sent her the treats and then came back to the city with a police officer to frame me for it since you knew how much I liked to bake. I caught you before you could carry out your plan, and you tried to kill me, as well. But unlike Blanche, I was able to turn the tables on you both. Now, this next part is up to you. Either you realized you'd been caught and committed suicide by eating the poisoned brownies you meant for me. Or, I shot and killed you both before you could do away with me the way you did Blanche."

There were holes in her story, but that didn't matter. She was a little old lady. People would already be hesitant to believe her capable of something as horrid as murder, so if she was able to introduce any doubt at all, there was no telling how people's opinions would be swayed.

"So, which ending do you prefer?" Mable asked, her shoulders noticeably shivering against the wind. "I hope you'll hurry and decide. I'm anxious to get back inside."

In the fading afternoon sun, Mable looked even more fragile than she had inside. Her skin was papery and dry, her hair frizzy and thinning. I could see liver spots on her scalp and the backs of her hands. Suddenly, it hit me that this woman would kill me. Even with Mable's lack of humanity on full display, I'd found it difficult to reconcile the kind woman I'd spoken to most days as I'd come and gone from the building with the scowling, gun-wielding woman in front of me. Mable had often felt like a grand-mother-like figure to me while I was away from my own grandparents. But now she looked like a monster. Her fears of leaving her apartment had twisted and molded her into a monster, and she would do whatever it took to be sure she wasn't afraid anymore.

"You know," Mable said, her pale lips twitching up into a smile. "I think I like the idea of being the hero. The news would love an elderly woman who stood her ground and fought off her attackers. Not only will I get away with it, but I'll be praised."

Tucker was sitting up now, his hands propped out to either side of him like the kickstand of a bike. I could see how hard he was fighting to regain full consciousness. As Mable spoke, his entire body seemed to tense, as if he could hear her and wanted to act, but his body couldn't move beyond the haze of whatever drugs Mable had given him. He looked helpless, like a small child, and I knew I couldn't let him die this way.

"Which one of you first?" Mable asked, shifting the gun back and forth between the two of us like a game of Eenie, Meenie, Miney, Mo. A cool wind blew across the top of the roof, lifting the fabric of Mable's floral dressing gown and tousling my hair. A few strands whispered across my face before settling behind my ear as though tucked there.

I lifted my hands in surrender and then took a large step forward, closing the distance between myself and the old woman by almost half. Now, she was only four feet away from me. Point blank range. If she had an opportunity to pull the trigger, it would be a miracle if she didn't hit me.

"Me," I said, studying Mable's every move. I was now close enough to her to lunge forward and fight for the gun, but I was waiting for the best opportunity. I needed Mable to be distracted enough that she wouldn't pull the trigger immediately. I needed an extra second.

"It makes no difference to me," Mable said, shifting her aim to me. I could see the short barrel of the weapon shivering in her grip, but it wouldn't be enough to cause Mable to miss. Her arms stiffened, as though preparing to shoot.

"Wait," I called out, holding a hand towards her.

Her eyes widened and then she sighed. "What is it?"

"Can I have a final moment with my thoughts?" I asked. "A prayer?"

I remembered seeing the large Bible on Mable's coffee table. Clearly, she'd never read it, but I hoped she was devout enough to respect my right to a prayer.

She nodded, and I knelt to one knee, my head lowered as if in prayer. But really, I was in a runner's stance. The foot next to my knee was tensed and ready to propel me forward, my hands were positioned on the ground on either side of my foot for balance. Adrenaline tingled up my arms and down my legs, preparing me to fight for mine and Tucker's lives. And really, I did say a quick prayer, asking that my attempt to take down Mable be successful. And then just as I took a deep breath and prepared to launch myself forward, a shiver started at the base of my neck and worked down my spine. It didn't feel like nerves or adrenaline. It felt like an unnatural chill. One I had become intimately familiar with.

I heard Mable inhale sharply. "What was that?"

When I looked up, Mable was spinning wildly in a circle, her head snapping back and forth to either side, causing her cheeks to shiver and shake like a gelatin mold in an earthquake.

"Who did that?" she asked, eyes wide and milky. "Who pushed me?"

For a brief moment, I smiled. Mable couldn't see what I could see. She didn't notice the soft blue shimmer circling around her—the middle-aged spirit still wearing the long dress and fake jewelry she'd worn during her life. Mable couldn't see that Blanche's eyes were narrowed and her jaw, once busy chewing the brownies that would end her life, was now set in determination.

I knew this was my opportunity. Blanche had drawn Mable's attention away long enough for me to act. I launched myself forward, my foot pushing off of the asphalt roof as my hands lifted from the ground and reached for the confused old woman.

Mable didn't react to me until my hands were on her arms. Mable looked fragile, but if it was possible, she felt even more fragile. Her skin was dry and soft like tissue paper and the bones beneath felt like they could belong to the birds she liked to punish. It took remarkably little effort for me to fling both her arms to the side, causing the gun to clatter to the ground at our feet.

Mable kicked out at me with a dark tan orthopedic shoe, connecting with my knee cap and making me groan. It wasn't enough to injure me, but it was enough to make me take one stumbling step backwards. It was enough to give Mable the extra second she needed to bend down and reclaim the gun. I watched as her hand wrapped around the black handle, as she straightened up, ready to pull the trigger without hesitation. And then, I watched as she was tossed sideways like a plastic bag in an icy wind, a wispy trail of blue smoke behind her.

Blanche's spirit pushed Mable the way I'd seen football players plow into stuffed dummies during football practice. It was like a train plowing into a car on the tracks. Even though we'd been standing in the center of the roof, Blanche somehow gathered the energy to pummel Mable all the way to the edge. The old woman's arms circled once for balance, trying to stop herself, but then she tipped over the side and disappeared. Blanche's glassy shape remained for another second before she too flicked away.

20

M able had been telling the truth. Tucker just needed a nap. The sleeping pills she'd slipped into the tea she gave him were powerful, but ultimately harmless. He woke up on my sofa.

"Tucker?" I held up a finger to Jay Wilkins, stopping him in the middle of his sentence. "Tucker are you okay?"

He sat up slowly, a hand pressed to his forehead. "What happened?"

I explained everything to him, revealing the details one at a time, waiting for him to nod his head in understanding before I moved on.

"I called the police from my cellphone as soon as Mable...fell off the edge, and then the EMTs carried you down here," I said. "We're supposed to take you to the emergency room if you wake up and feel at all strange."

"I feel like I'm still dreaming," he said. "Does that count as feeling strange?"

I smiled. "I think I'd be more concerned if you didn't feel that way."

Jay, in a surprisingly thoughtful move, walked over with a glass of water, and Tucker drank the whole thing almost immediately.

"Worst case of cotton mouth ever," he said, smacking his lips together.

"Do you remember what happened?" I asked.

He closed his eyes, wrinkled his forehead, and then opened them, nodding. "Bits and pieces. I was lookin' for you," he said, tipping his head towards me. "I wanted to apologize about earlier and let you know I planned to stay in the city until you were ready to leave, but I couldn't get ahold of you. I was about to leave when Mable opened the front door for me. She told me I could wait in her apartment for you, and since I knew you were friendly with Mable, I thought I could trust her."

"I thought you could, too," I said, shaking my head, still in disbelief.

"She offered me some tea, but I said no thanks. I've never been a big tea drinker," he said. "But she made it for me anyway, and I felt rude refusing, so I drank half the mug. Right away, my head started to swim, and by the time I thought it could have been the tea, it was too late. The effects came on too quickly for me to do much of anything. Mable pushed me back into the sofa and said she would take care of me. And that's the last thing I remember."

"She tried to take care of you, all right," Jay said. His mouth was turned down in a scowl. "She tried to take care of you both just like she took care of my mother."

Jay's face was red, his jaw clenched. I reached out and patted his arm. He stiffened at my touch and then offered me a smile before stepping out of my reach. "I owe you both for solving the murder. I would have continued living below that woman without the slightest idea that she had killed my mother."

"I was unconscious for all of it," Tucker said. "You should thank Emma."

I shrugged. "It was nothing, really. Mostly it was an accident."

Jay shook his head. "No, it wasn't. You set out to solve the case, and you did it better than the police. My mom wasn't always an easy woman to live with, but she didn't deserve the end she got. So, thank you for putting this whole thing to rest."

"Of course," I said, hoping Jay was right. I wanted Blanche to find peace, and I hoped that by pushing her killer off the top of the building, she'd found that. When the police had arrived, they confirmed that Mable was dead. I'd watched them load her body into the back of the ambulance, a blanket thrown over her.

"Well," Jay said, looking noticeably uncomfortable. "I guess I should let the two of you rest. You've had a pretty big day. Let me know if there's anything else you need."

Without waiting for a reply, Jay turned to leave, looking eager to escape our presence.

"Actually, there is something I wanted to ask you," I said calling after him.

Jay turned back around reluctantly, his shoulders sagging with disappointment at this encounter being prolonged. "Yes?"

"I remember you mentioning something about your mother having a cat," I said.

He nodded. "Pudding."

The cat's name was Pudding? Not great, but I could work with that.

"You also mentioned you were allergic?"

He nodded again. "Very. I break out in hives with prolonged contact."

"Well, my grandparents have farmland in Missouri, and I love animals. I was wondering if you would be willing to let me take...Pudding...home with me? I know she was your mother's cat, and you might want—"

"He," Jay said. "Pudding is a boy."

"Right, of course," I said with a smile. "Well, I know *he* was your mother's cat, but I love animals and don't have an allergy, so—"

"He's yours," Jay said.

"Really?"

"Absolutely. It's a relief honestly. I would've felt bad taking him to a shelter, but I can't stand to be around him for more than five minutes without my entire body starting to itch." Jay scratched his stomach at just the memory of his allergic reaction. "I think my mom bought him just to keep an eye on me. It ensured she had to come down to my apartment several nights a week for dinner, so she got to inspect how clean my place was and whether there were any signs of me doing anything she wouldn't approve of."

I decided to ignore the awkward part about Jay and his mother, and instead just thanked him.

"I'll unlock the door and you can take Pudding and all of his stuff before you go," he said.

I also decided not to tell Jay that his mother's apartment door was already unlocked from my investigation earlier.

As soon as he left, I turned around to see Tucker shaking his head.

"Are you feeling alright?" I asked. "Does your head hurt?"

"No, I'm fine. Just ready to be home," he said. After a long pause he ran a hand through his hair. "Life in the big city is a bit more than I bargained for. Murderous neighbors, warring mother/son landlords. Hillbilly Hollow is nothing compared to even the drama in this one building."

I laughed, thinking that Tucker didn't even know about the hacker on the fifth floor who once broke into the databases of the National Security Agency. And I intended to leave it that way.

Then, my phone buzzed. It was a text from Billy, but before I could even respond to the first one, several more buzzed in.

BILLY: R U okay?

BILLY: Am I mistaken, or is your apartment building on the news?

BILLY: Yes, I've been following the New York City news since U left. No, that does not make me crazy.

WE WERE ON THE NEWS? Part of me wanted to look, but a more dominant part of me thought it would be best to let it go. Whatever was being reported was either wrong, or if it wasn't, I already knew the story. There was no sense in stressing Tucker out more, anyway. He looked exhausted, and not just from the sleeping pills.

ME: Remember how I said I'd tell U everything over shakes at the diner?

BILLY: Yes. U better not be backing out. I want to hear everything.

ME: I will tell U everything, but we may have to extend it to a three-course meal.

BILLY: Cheese fries for appetizer, burgers for main, shakes for dessert.

ME: U've got yourself a deal. I'm on the first flight out tomorrow morning.

BILLY: Thank goodness. Be safe until then.

ME: Always.

WHEN I LOOKED up from my phone, Tucker had fallen asleep again on the couch, his head lolled back on the cushion, mouth open. I smiled and draped my fleece throw blanket over him before sneaking away and heading downstairs to Blanche's apartment. I wanted to spend as much time with Pudding as possible before our flight the next morning.

As I walked down the familiar hallways and stairwells, I realized how little I would miss the old brick building I'd once called home. Maybe the time had finally come to give up my old apartment for good and stop keeping a foot in both worlds—New York and Missouri. Even though I had my own furniture and space here, my apartment didn't seem near as inviting as the attic space in my grandparents' house. Plus, New York City may have been home to over eight million people, but it didn't have Billy Stone or Suzy Colton. Or even a Sheriff Larry Tucker. Hillbilly Hollow had my grandparents, who I couldn't wait to see again. And Snowball. It had kind people and a small-town charm I realized I couldn't live without.

And, as much as I'd fought it at first, Hillbilly Hollow was sure to have more ghostly adventures in store for me. I smiled, finding myself looking forward to them.

CONTINUE FOLLOWING *the ghostly mysteries and eccentric characters of Hillbilly Hollow in "A Haunted Holiday in Hillbilly Hollow."*

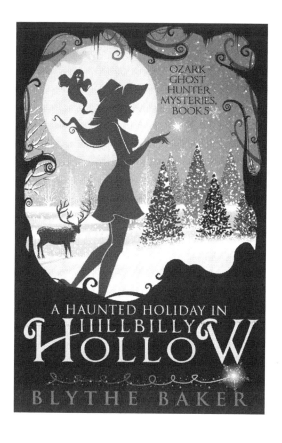

Made in the USA
Middletown, DE
04 April 2020